The Broken Man

By Andrew Furr

Edited by Dawn-Moree Duggan

Dedicated

Dedicated to those who run in to danger at their own peril to help those in desperate need. Those who deal with aftershock of traumatic events. Those who are broken afterwards and still work and fight to continue on the path.

A special thanks to my friend Dawn-Moree for all your help in my life. People like you make the world truly a better place.

Table of Content

CHAPTER 1

THAT DAY

A detective slowly moves through a low-lit boiler room. Cautious and methodically he makes his way, aiming his weapon at every possible place. Danger could jump out at him. He begins to hear through the machinery, sounds of a whimper. As he moves closer, she comes into view. Sally Ann, she's blindfolded, gagged and tied to a table. Her feet are blood-soaked. In between each of her toes is a thin deep cut. Nothing that could kill her, but it would torture the body and mind.

Sally had been missing for a week. Detective Jova Zarn was determined no more were going to die. Sally was the sixth victim. The killer would keep the victims alive for 10 days, according to the Medical Examiner. The speculation was that he would use mental torture and then lead up to bodily torture. First there would be small cuts all over, then live amputations, until death finally came for the victim. Two never made it through the small cuts. They could no longer take it and just gave up.

The detective had worked on terrible cases before. He tended to get more intensely focused as the case went on, to the point of having no private life of any kind. He was going to stop this killer no matter what it took. He looked greasy and unclean. He had two weeks of whiskers that covered his face. As he made his way to the sounds of Sally. Carefully he surveyed the room. One light was directly over her. Large steam pipes and all kinds of different machinery faded off to darkness. He can hardly keep from rushing to her.

He does not know where the killer is. He puts his hand softly over her mouth. He places his gun on the table. He removes her blindfold, then quietly whispers in her ear. "Sally-Ann, I'm detective Jova Zarn, please don't make a sound. I'm going to get you out of here. I need you to be as quiet as you can, Ok?". Tears flood her eyes as she nods her head. Her lips quiver as he takes the gag off. Small whimpering breaths come uncontrollably from her. "Please, Sally, try to be quiet", he whispers to her. She stares into his eyes and nods as tears continue to stream from her eyes.

Jova releases her one arm then the other. She grabs on to him hugging him, burying her face into his chest crying and whimpering. He undoes her feet and pushes her back to see her face. Whispering to her "Listen to me very carefully. I'm going to carry you out of here. Try not to make a sound". She nods her head yes. He quietly askes," Did you see who did this to you?" She nods her head again. A look of fear comes over her face. "Sally, Sally okay, okay I know, I know" he pleads with her.

He says "I don't know where the killer is. All I want to do is get you out of here." She takes a whimpering breath and nods. "If anything happens to me, I want you to run, run no matter what you feel or see or hear. Get out of this place and find a policeman. Okay, Sally okay?" She stares at him, tearing up, realizing this nightmare is not over. "No matter what happens, you run." Jova shakes her as he says it. She nods. Up over his shoulder, he drapes her, holding the backs of her legs with one hand and his gun in the other.

He tries to move cautiously. The killer could be anywhere down there. He knows Sally needs to get out of there no matter what happens. He begins to walk faster and faster. Finally, the exit sign over the stairway door comes into view. She starts whimpering uncontrollably. He stops about 20 feet from the doorway and stands her upright and says with concern "Hang on Sally we are almost out." He looks back and sees nothing. He turns to her and tries to be reassuring and says, "Sally you are doing good, girl you are doing very good."

She stares into his eyes and sees his deepest sincerity as he tries to give her a little pep talk. He holsters his gun and takes his coat off. "Sally let's put this jacket on you. We don't want you catching a cold now do we?" she shakes her head no. He zips up the jacket and asks if that's better. She nods her head yes. He takes his thumb and wipes her cheeks off. "You are doing real good Sally."

He squats down and picks her up over his shoulder again. He walks to the exit door. He looks behind him one last time. He grasps the door handle slowly and he pushes the door open. As he steps through the threshold a knife jams into the front of his right thigh. A loud groan comes from clenched teeth. A gloved hand rips it back out and stabs him again in the same thigh. Jova breathes in deeply with teeth clenched tightly. The gun falls to the floor and Jova's stance crumbles and Sally falls out of the way to the floor.

The killer tries for another stab. Jova grabs the knife hand and goes down to his knees. Sally grasps the handrail as her tail hits the stairs. Fear covers her face and her eyes go wide, as she realizes what's happening. In slow motion, she stares at Jova's face. He stares back and yells" RUN SALLY RUN "!

She pulls herself upright and starts running up the stairs. Her feet leave bloody footprints with every step up the stairs. Her feet go numb as she runs. She whimpers but never screams. The light gets brighter and brighter with each step. No sound, just a thump of her heart. Thump, thump, thump, as she moves up into the bright light of daylight, all her senses make her feel like she is moving in slow-motion, just the thump, thump, thump, of her heartbeat. The door to the outside was in view. Jova's voice comes into her head in a soft whisper "Find a cop, find a cop, you are doing good, very good". The outside air hits her face. Thump, thump, thump pulsing over her whole body.

Her heartbeats are the only sound she hears. She emerges from the door into an alley. She looks both ways - to the right trash containers overflowing with garbage - to the left cars and people moving back and forth into view. She runs for the people thump, thump, thump. Find a cop, find a cop' Jova's voice ran through her head. The world moves slowly as each step hits the ground. Hundreds of people fill the sidewalks of the city. She arrives at the sidewalk. People stop and stare. A woman moves toward her in slow motion, yelling, "HELP HER!!! HELP HER!!!"

Sally's knees buckle under her. The people seem frozen in time. A man and a woman break free from their frozen stance and move towards Sally. Three other people overcome their stunned disbelief and start yelling "police, POLICE, POLICE". Sally looks up at the people and says "HELP JOVA, PLEASE, HELP HIM" as her eyes close. Silence fills her head as darkness engulfs her world. Two uniformed police officers come to the crowd. They radio for backup and EMTs.

One policeman takes his jacket off and covers her with it. One woman cradled her head in her lap. The other woman held Sally's hand and the man whipped his sports coat off and wrapped it around her feet. The police asked, if she's okay. The woman cradling her said that she's still breathing. The policeman says, "Look after her. The EMT's will be here in a few minutes."

The two policemen follow the bloody footprints down the alley. One officer reports on his radio, "We are making entry at 2056 West street, south alley entrance, two uniforms investigating an assault on a woman." A reply comes back "Roger, David 18, assistance 2 minutes out." "Roger," he replies. Their weapons were drawn and flashlights out. They work their way down the stairs, following the bloody footprints.

Sounds of grunting and growling get louder and closer. The bottom stair landing was covered in fresh blood. One officer pulls the door open as the other enters. "FREEZE DON'T MOVE!" the policeman yells. A man straddles another with a knife in his hands raised up over his head. Ready to plunge it down into the unconscious man. The knife starts to move downward. "BLAM, BLAM, BLAM! " The sound of gunfire blast deafens everyone there. The knife falls from his hands as he slumps over.

Jova's eyes slowly crack open to a great light. A gurgling sound first comes from his lips. After a spit of bloody fluids, he whispers out "Is she okay? IS SHE OKAY?" The policeman answers him slowly "She is safe, detective. Don't worry she is safe, and this piece of shit is dead. You don't worry detective just hang on". The darkness of quiet covers him. Sirens and lights fade away, as various paramedics work to stabilize him for transport.

Like coming out of a deep pool of water. Jova starts to hear and see small snapshots of masked faces and voices. "More whole blood ... get that bleeder and clamp it off". Then silence and darkness take over again.

Days later Jova's eyes slightly open. In a dimly lit hospital room, a blurry figure is leaning over him. He quickly grabs at the figure and starts yelling "run, RUN, RUN" as he fades off again. A nurse yells from the room

"I need help, help now!!! He broke open some sutures." A doctor and two nurses run in to help. An hour goes by as all the wounds are dressed.

The doctor asked what happened. The nurse answers "I was checking his temp and he grabbed me and started yelling." The doctor asked, what he had say? The nurse replied "He kept yelling run, run, run. What does it mean doctor?" The doctor answered "He might have been reliving the nightmare that brought him here. I guess we will have to ask him when and if he wakes up again. For now, just sedate and restrain him until he gets stable. He surely won't wake up if he bleeds out. Keep a close eye on him."

Three days pass and the nurse rolls Sally Ann into the room, with her feet all bandaged. The nurse says "He came to for a couple of seconds three days ago. He grabbed me and was yelling run, run. He scared the hell out of me."

Sally took a deep breath "That's the last thing he said to me" she said with a gasp of concern. "Oh?" said the nurse. Feeling that she wanted a moment alone with, Jova the nurse said, "I'll be back in about thirty minutes sweetie. Just don't excite him, we can't have him jumping around breaking open his wounds." Sally never took her eyes from Jova as she answered, "Yes nurse, I will be quiet and calm."

She looks over him, slowly, seeing over 500 stitches throughout his body and face. White bandages covered his legs, arms, and face. His vest protected a lot of his chest and abdomen, but not his arms and legs and face. She grasped his hand gently and said "Thank you, detective Jova Zarn. Thank you so much. No one ever sacrificed or did so much for me." Tears covered her flushed cheeks.

She bowed her head down, "Dear God please bless this brave, brave man. Thank you for guiding him to save me. Please God if I have any favors from you, please bless them upon him. Thank you. He deserves so much. Please watch over him." She places her forehead against his hand. "Bless you, Jova Zarn and you get well. The world needs men like you."

A week goes by and Jova awakens. The doctor examines him and says "Well, Jova you seem to be healing fine. Your blood count seems to be coming into normal levels now. I'm going to allow you more movement, but just very mild and light." Jova asked, "Can I go to the bathroom doc?" "Let's see how you do. Just move slowly and if you feel anything pulling just stop."

"Ok, doc." The doctor helps him up to his feet. The doctor inquires, how that feels? "Some pins and needles in my legs Jova replies with a grim look of discomfort on his face. The doc tells him to take a small step and stop, then take another small step, then asked how he felt now? The same, doc, a little like my legs fell asleep." "Alright, two steps and that's it, ok two more there you go, you're moving now. Through the bathroom door, you go. How do you feel now?" Jova says "Like I need about 15 minutes of some alone time doc." "Alright, there is a pull switch for help in there. Don't hesitate to call, because if you break your sutures open, it will set back recovery time." "Okay, doc ok." The doctor tells him, through the closed door, that he I will check back in after a while and leaves.

A couple of days go by. Jova adds a little more walking in each day. He moved at a slow pace with a limp in his right leg. As he walked past the nurse's station, a nurse would say," Who is that masked man? Is it the Lone Ranger?"

The doctor comes in and asks Jova how he is doing. "Good Doc, good." The Doctor answered "Ok." The doctor told him that he was going to remove the face bandages. He slowly unraveled and snipped with his scissors. Jova's patience was wearing thin as he encouraged the doctor to hurry up, "Come on doc let's get it done. You know it itches like hell." The doctor removes them and tells him that everything looks like its healing very well.

"Now when you start shaving yourself take your time. You have some different contours to your face now. This ointment I'm applying to your face, should cut back on the irritation and promote faster healing time. I should be able to take the stitches out in a couple more days. The nurse comes in and asked, how Jova was doing. "My face stopped itching." "That's good" she replied. As she talks Jova notices she doesn't have the same eye contact. It was a forced eye contact and then she would look quickly away. She excused herself and left.

The doctor asked, "Alright how are your legs doing any numbness or odd sensations?" "No doc they seem to be pretty good, a little tight sometimes." The Doctor kept looking him over and told him that he was doing well, that everything seemed to be healing properly. Jova asked, "Doc when do you think I'll be discharged?" "If nothing changes, right after I take your stitches out in two days. Now don't do anything different. No strenuous movements." Jova reassures the doctor, "Ok doc."

Jova lies in the bed thinking about the nurse's reaction. From that point on he only does his walking at night. When people are in sight he turns toward the walls. He uses his IV stand to block his face from view. Two days pass and the doctor takes all the stitches out. "Everything still okay Jova? No problems, no unusual pains, numbness?" Jova answers with a sense of urgency in his voice, "No doc, I'm ready to get out of here, no offense, but I'm getting a little stir crazy." The doctor says "I can understand that. You are clear as far as I'm concerned, just let me get the rest of these stitches out." Jova thanks the doc and asked, "How is Sally Ann doing? Is she still here?"

"No Jova, we transferred her to a psychiatric facility. She came to visit you several times, but you were unconscious the first week. She made everyone pray for you that whole week. She stayed in the hospital chapel most of her stay here. I never saw anything like it before. She even got me going back to church. I barely went before this and especially not during football season." He laughed. "She is with a good doctor who is very good with traumatic events." Jova heaved a sigh of relief, "Good doc. Sally is a good person she didn't deserve to be tainted by such an evil bastard." The doctor concurred and added, "You saved her from a quite horrific situation."

Jova answered humbly, "I know doc. I just wish I could have stopped him before the other five died." The doctor agreed and said, "Well Jova that's the last one. Keep everything clean, nothing strenuous and take all those antibiotics." Jova perked up knowing he was getting out of there and he thanked the doctor and the nurses for all their help and care.

The doctor said in a serious voice, "A lot of cops are my most hard- headed patients. So please, please Jova take it easy and allow yourself time to heal properly." "I will doc" Jova answered while he was gathering his personal effects. He wasted no time getting out of there.

CHAPTER 2

SALLY IS A COMING

Three days later, Sally-Ann is at the police station. She was led to an interrogation room by a uniformed officer who told her to just have a seat, and a detective would be with her in a moment. "Yes sir," she politely answers. The door opens and a sharp suit-wearing man enters the room. As he turns, she smiles for a moment and then goes straight-faced. The detective introduces himself in a perfunctory manner and tone, "I'm detective Sam Winters, I'm glad you could come in today." She said, "Excuse me, I thought detective Jova would be here."

He replied, while looking down at the files, he's not back from medical leave yet. "I thought he was discharged from the hospital", she said with concern. The detective answered with little concern in his demeanor, "He was, I believe he is at home recuperating."

Sally said, with care, "Oh his family is looking after him - that's good." He replied casually, "He doesn't have any family that I'm aware of Miss Sally." With a sad tone, she questioned his statement, "No wife or even a girlfriend?" Sally's voice became stern, "Oh no, that won't do not at all. I'll need his address, so I can bring him some things. The detective finally made eye contact with her face and said, "Ma'am, I can't give out a detective's home address." She quickly asked why not, and he answered with a tone of discontent "It's against policy and it protects his privacy." "Nonsense", she snapped back at him. He said "Miss, I just had you come in, to finish writing up this report." She quickly said "Well, I'm not saying anything until I get his address and that's final." He pleaded "Miss, please be reasonable." Sally just stared at him. He pleaded again "Please, Miss, I can't leave until I get this statement done." Sally, said to the detective, "I'm in a hurry, I have somewhere I am supposed to be." He asked, "Where is that, Miss?" She said with determination, "I don't know - you haven't given me the address!!" The detective rubs his face with both hands and pleaded, "Pretty, please with sugar on top." She just stared at him. He harshly wrote on a piece of paper, ripped it out of his small folding notebook and slammed it on the table. "That's all I know. I don't know the exact address, but this will get you there. Now I know how suspects feel," he said with great frustration. She read the paper and smiled with great satisfaction. A big smile adorned her face. "How may I help you, detective", she asked? He stared at her for a minute. Then he shook off his signs of frustration. He Smiled insincerely. "Ok Miss Sally Ann, tell me what happened starting with the night you were abducted." She gasped, "Oh!" and she starts rummaging through her big black purse.

"Here it is. The doctor had me write everything down. You know while it was still fresh. Plus, this symbolized me taking that terrible event out of me, so we could work out getting past it." The detective read through the pages. "Oh, this will do fine, just fine. I just need you to sign here and here." She signs. He was glad his task was complete and asked with some concern and care, "So, do you feel you are past it?" She replied softly, "No, but I do feel a little better." "Well, Miss Sally Ann, you take care and thank you for your statement." The detective opened the door and concluded by asking an officer that was nearby to show her out. "Thank you." The detective sat back down and read the papers. That's all he needed to get this all wrapped up. He smiled as he placed all his paperwork under his arm and strolled out with great confidence.

Sally wasted no time. She stopped at her apartment, got a couple of bags packed, almost stumbling with them, and tossed them in the back of her little car. She drove out of town with a great smile on her face. Then the smile went away. She thought to herself, if that man gave me the wrong directions to trick me, I'll go back there and kick him right in his fruity patootie.

She continued with her happy thoughts of helping Jova and seeing him again to thank him. She drove out of the city. The landscape changed to a very rural setting. Lots of farmland with horses and cows grazing in the fields. She pulled into a small grocery store where the direction's led her. She entered the store with great confidence and grabbed a cart. She went up and down the aisles thinking to herself, about the many great meals she could make.

As she was checking out, she asked the clerk,

"Do you know where Jova Zarn lives?" The older man smiled and answered, "Well yes, are you a friend of his?" She said with a smile, "I sure am, and all of this is for him." He looked at her and all the items. The clerk, with a bit of envy in his voice, said "Well then you are a good friend." and he laughed. "He's been getting those blasted tv dinner things. I sell them, but between you and me I think they are nasty. My son was just getting a delivery order together for Jova. You can follow him up the road." "Peck" he yells to the back of the store. A young boys voice answers, "Yes Pops?" A lanky 14-year-old boy walks up and comes to the counter. Sally asked, "What is Peck short for?" The clerk spoke up, "That is what I call him. His name is Montgomery Taylor. My wife loved Montgomery Cliff, but I was a fan of Gregory Peck." Sally smiled as she listens to the clerk continue, "We almost went with naming him after Chuck Heston, but then the thought of naming him after a shoe sounded like a bad idea. So, as all great decisions go in my family, the wife won. As a consolation prize, I got to nickname him Peck. The boy just quietly looked down, trying not to show embarrassment. "Peck, you let this nice lady follow you over to Mr. Zarn's place." The young man answered respectfully, "Yes Pops. I'll pull around the front in a couple of minutes, Miss." Peck ran to the back of the store. The clerk continued talking to Sally as he walked her out and put the groceries in her car.

The clerk said with great pride, Yeah, I didn't want the boy to be embarrassed so I call him Peck, you know like in the movies; The Gunfighter, To Kill a Mockingbird, The Yellow Sky." That was a man's, man. A stern woman's voice came from the door, "Red River, Raintree County and From Here to Eternity." A petite woman in her fifties playfully smiled at him from the doorway.

He said with great admiration in his voice, "That's my Princess Ann she has had my heart on a scooter ride all my life. I have been on a Roman holiday for 25 years now." The lady blushed and covered her mouth. "Stop it!" She said in a soft voice. He interjected, "This woman is a friend of Jova's." The woman said, "Nice to meet you." She came away from the door to shake Sallie's hand. "He's a good boy don't you go breaking his heart now." "I won't," said Sally with a warm smile.

A little horn sounded," Beep, Beep" as Peck rides up, on an old Vespa scooter with a wooden box on the back. The clerk says, "There is my boy, you just follow him, and you'll be there in no time, and tell Jova to stop by some time soon. We haven't seen him in a couple of months." "Ok, I will, bye, bye," Sally said. Sally thought that was the sweetest couple. He could still make his wife blush after so many years. It brought a warm feeling over her.

She followed Peck down the curvy small road. It soon turned in to a dirt road. They were only 45 minutes from one of the largest cities in the U.S. and now nothing but trees and fields of corn, cows, goats, and horses.

She remembered as a kid going on a field trip to a

petting zoo, where they let her pet the animals and feed the chickens. It was so exciting to her as a little kid. She touched a sheep, goat, and pig. She even got to sit on a pony for 5 minutes. Sally was giddy with memories of that fun time she had.

Trees lined both sides of the road now. Finally, a small clearing came into view and an old farmhouse with a wrap-around porch. It even had a two-person swing hanging on it. A big wooden barn stood beside the house.

Several old trucks parked and decaying beside the barn. In front of the house, was one old truck, all clean and shiny, like it was just off the showroom floor, forty years ago. A hound dog lay at the top of the steps almost blocking the whole walkway, brown and black with a white chin and chest, droopy ears and a sad face. A couple of sniffs at Peck and a tired half-hearted try at a "woof "at Peck as he walked up to the stairs to the front door was all he could manage. Peck placed the bag on the porch and rang the doorbell.

As he turned the hound rolled on to its side. Peck bent over to give his tummy a couple of rubs. Peck came down the steps and walked over to Sally's car and said, "This is it, he is around here somewhere. He never answers the door lately. I just leave the bag by the front door. You want me to help you carry your bags in? She gleefully replied, "Oh yes, please, and does that dog bite?" Peck playfully answered, "Not if you give his tummy a rub here and there. That's 'The Dude' or mostly just Dude. Come on I'll introduce you."

As they approached Dude's eyes were following them. His head raised up just a little bit, and he took a couple of sniffs, then his head slumped back to the porch. Peck carried two bags up the stairs and Sally followed closely behind with one bag. Peck opened the front door and walked in and placed the bags on the kitchen table while Sally stood at the front door, so Peck took the last bag from her. Sally turned and kneeled and gave a vigorous rub to the dog's belly and said, "Hello Mr. Dude I'm Sally." His leg stretched outward and a nice relaxed groan came from Dude. His tail wagged several times slapping on to the porch. Peck smiled and said, "I guess y'all are good friends now." "I imagine Mr. Zarn will be back soon. Our number is on the bags if you need anything. Nice to meet you." He jumps on his scooter and rides away, a little trail of dust clouding the driveway as he putters out of site. She looks off the porch, rubbing Dudes belly.

The sun was falling behind the trees. She thought it's rather peaceful back in here with no horns beeping, no hustle and bustle, no smell of gas fumes, no sirens, no angry people yelling 'get a move on or get out of the way'. Even the birds were chirping as they hopped about getting their evening supper.

Sally made herself busy cleaning up in the kitchen. Putting groceries away and evaluating how little he had in his refrigerator. It was a man's kitchen now, but a woman had been here in the past. Pots and pans were hidden under the cabinets. There was an assortment of spices, a little bit on the old side, but still workable.

While she was cooking, the bedroom door cracked open and an eye peered through it. A man's voice came through the crack of the door sounding tired and irritable. "Who's here, Peck is that you? Go on home, I'll pay the bill tomorrow. Go on, I don't want to be bothered." Sally answered the voice, "It's not Peck, and get yourself washed up, dinners almost ready." Jova with puzzlement asked, "Who are you?"

Sally was quiet for a moment and started to feel a little nervous. She took a deep breath and said, "It's me, Sally Ann, so get washed up for dinner." Jova was nervous in his reply and said, "That's nice and everything, but you don't need to do that." He stumbled around in his room pulling up his pants. His room was a mess, with clothes all over the floor and his bed unmade, with blankets hanging off to the floor. His hair was long and unkempt. He pulled an old sweatshirt on.

Sally continued preparing the plates. "Ok dinners ready. Come and get it." He stood in the room trying to figure a way out of seeing her. Rubbing his face and scratching his head he tried once again to convince her to leave saying, "I think it would be better if---". Sally barked out "I'm not leaving until I see you eat at least one good meal. Come on, move your patootie. It is ready."

He took a deep breath, gripped the doorknob and he pulled the door open slowly. The creaking door hinges rang through the house. Sally smiled as she sat down, at the table. He kept his head down as he walked to the kitchen and sat down. The smell of the food was fantastic. His house normally had a lingering musty smell, but the smell of freshly cooked food now filled the air. His hands shook a little from nerves. He looked up into her eyes and she was focused dead on him.

A big smile came over her "I'm so happy to see you." She never glanced away as she continued to speak, "I wanted to see you at the hospital, but the psychiatrist wanted me to stay to keep working through, the thing, you know. So, I kept working, but I swore that when I was out of there, I would come and look you up and thank you."

He asked, "How did you get my address?" She cheerfully replied, "Oh, at the police station," she said proudly. He was put back and said, "They are not supposed to do that." Sally said, "I know, they said that several times. Finally, I met the detective Sam Winters. He was a bit hard-headed, at first, but he came around. Then I met the grocery store people, they were lovely. They wished their best to you and wanted you to come by soon to catch up." Jova looked at her as she talked about everything. She never slowed down, she never looked away from him. He gave up trying to join the conversation, but he did enjoy listening to her talk. She noticed things about the world and the people that he had become oblivious too.

He ate the food and it was the best meal he had in years. Oven-baked chicken, corn and peas mixed together, mashed potatoes and biscuits with a sweet tea chaser.

Sometimes he would relax and not think about himself and what he had been through. Her voice was soft and flowed gently into his mind. She talked about her mom teaching her how to cook. She had taught her how to make this very meal and her dad loved it. "My mother always said it is better to know how to cook something well. She said no matter where you go or what you do eventually you are going to need to eat and here, we are. There is plenty more, too. Do you want seconds?" Jova's belly was full, which was no hard achievement. His appetite had been low on his priorities and his stomach had shrunk. He spoke up and said, "No Ma'am, but don't throw it away, I will want more tomorrow. I have some plastic containers in the cabinet over the sink. I'll get them." She quickly jumped up and said, "No silly, I'm running this show." She went to the sink and reached up and realized she was a tad short of her task. She turned and lightly bit her lip and just cleared her throat "ah hum". Jova gave a small grin as he rose from his seat. He moved with apprehension. She stood at the sink following his movement toward her closer and closer, until his chest was close enough for her breath to push on his shirt fabric. She stood like a statue and her breath seemed to stop. His arms descended beside her. Abruptly a WOOF, WOOF came from the front door. Plastic containers and lids flew all over the counter and floor. They both awkwardly knelt down to pick up the lids and containers. An uncomfortable silence filled the room.

Jova said "Sounds like Dude, is ready for his dinner." Sally opened the door and Dude took a sniff at her and then strolled on in. Jova filled his dinner bowl with dog food. Dude sauntered over and flopped down with the bowl in between his front paws and proceeded to slowly eat. Jova knelt and began picking up containers and lids. Sally looked over at Dude, while he ate and said, "He certainly has some personality to him. I never had a dog, or really a pet of any kind." She began picking up around the kitchen while she talked. "I'll get this taken care of you go ahead and sit down."

"I do remember going to the petting zoo. Seeing the goats, chickens and some sheep. Have you ever looked at a goat's eyes? They are wild looking. They are not like people's eyes. They gave us some cracked corn to feed the chickens and ducks. I must have been in elementary school then." She nervously continued talking as she was putting everything away. Her subjects changed quite frequently and never a long enough of a break for Jova to answer or join in. He was fine with that. He was contented just watching her and listening to her talk.

She asked, "How have you been? Are you feeling ok? You sure don't talk a lot. I had an uncle like that. He would come over for a family dinner. He would greet you and stuff like that and the usual pleasantries. As we were all jabbering away in the kitchen, he would sneak off into the living room, and sit back in the easy chair. He would just close his eyes and take a nap. When I was little, I would try to sneak up on him. I would be on his chest staring at him. He would act like he did not feel me climbing on him. He would open his eyes. Excitedly he would say, 'There you are. I've been looking all over for you. Where have you been? I went to the great pyramids and you weren't there.' I would tell him I was right here. Then he would say 'I went to the Eiffel tower and you weren't there.' 'I was here you silly.' I would tell him giggling. He continued with, 'I went to the top of Mount Everest and looked all over for you.' 'I was here you silly!' 'Well, it is a good thing you showed up when you did. You see my hearts been feeling a little chilly today. I needed a heart warmer like you.' He would hug me tight. I could hear his heart beating. The others would be so loud talking away in the other room and he would just lay there with his eyes closed smiling.

Sally was in a constant state of busyness while she continued talking, washing dishes and wiping down the counters and table. She moved like a waitress at a busy diner.

Jova enjoyed listening to her. The tone of her voice was very warm and relaxing, like a hidden melody playing in the background. She stopped for a moment and was facing Jova and quiet came over the room. The silence seemed to last for minutes. Then Sally blurted out, "OOOOOOOOh MY", as Dude rubbed his nose on her bare leg. "Dude your nose it is so cold." She rubbed his side, "Oh who's got the cold nose? Who's got the cold nose? You do, you do," she said excitedly. His tail wagged.

Jova opened the front door and then sat down on the couch. Dude strolled out to the edge of the porch. He sniffed toward the left and then towards the right.

Sally stood next to the door watching Dude as he sauntered around the yard. "He certainly is in no hurry wherever he goes." She turned to Jova for a response. He was asleep, just sitting there. She peered at him as she came to the rear of the couch. A small amount of sweat appeared on his brow. She placed her hand on his forehead, and thought to herself, you are a little on the warm side.

On the kitchen counter, there were some prescription bottles. It was the same antibiotics she had to take. She got a couple of the pills and a glass of water. In a quiet voice said, "Jova take these pills." He leaned forward while still half asleep, took the pills and drank down some water. He leaned back. Then leaned over sideways and placed his head onto a pillow that was already there. A blanket lay across the back of the couch, so she covered him up with it.

She went back to his bedroom door and slowly pushed it open. Clothes were everywhere, on the floor, in a chair and some on the bed. A blanket was hanging half off the bed and on the floor. She said, "Well someone surely doesn't have a cleaning disorder here." She gladly began picking up clothes. She found the washing machine. She was surprised there was some washing detergent. She even found a linen closet with a change of sheets, so she stripped down the bed.

About several hours had gone by. She went to the couch and felt his head. "You're still warm sweetie, please take these pills." He would lean up enough to take the pills and water. She went back to making up the bed. The room was taking shape. She sat on the bed folding and sorting clothes that she had already washed and dried.

Finally, she laid back on to the bed and thought mmmmmmmmm fresh sheets always feel so good. She closed her eyes. The sunlight came across her body up until it shined on her face. Her eyes opened. She had worked through the night with no rest.

Jova slowly began to stir. Sounds of a jingling found his ears. It was a familiar sound he had heard every morning while he was growing up. It was the sound his grandmother made when she was stirring her morning coffee. The metal spoon was hitting the sides of the china cup. He never knew if she was aware of how much that sound rang through the house every morning. Grandpa drank it black, so you knew every time grandma was having coffee.

The smell of sizzling bacon filled his nose. His eyes opened as he took in a big sniff. Mmmmmmmm he thought. He stood up and turned toward the kitchen. "Good morning" she said with great warmth. "It smells like a wonderful morning" he replied. He poured himself a coffee and several sips later he was done. He poured another and sat down at the table. She said, "Right after breakfast, someone is taking a shower. Then they are getting a haircut." She spun around with a plate in her hand. "Aren't we?" She held the plate in front of him but did not let go until he replied. A veiled threat was implied. The plate had bacon, eggs and home fries with onions. He looked up at her and answered, "Why yes, yes, they are going to do anything you ask." She released the plate and smiled confidently. "The right answer" she said.

He ate like a wild animal tearing through the meal. He would try not to eat so fast, but it was so good. She looked on with astonishment as he ate and said, "Well, that reaction is a vote of confidence in my cooking abilities." He wiped his mouth and said that was great. She handed him two pills. He tossed them in his mouth and he drank down his coffee. He slowly got up and said, "I guess someone is going to take a shower now." She stopped him and said, "First the haircut. So that way you can wash the hair clipping's off." She placed a chair in the middle of the kitchen and he sat down. She draped a towel around him and she pulled a plastic box out of her purse. She started cutting and clumps of hair started hitting the floor. A bit of nervousness raced through him as he saw the hair clumps falling. He just closed his eyes and listened to her voice.

She told him, "I use to cut hair for a while. I'm not licensed though I was a shampoo girl at a beauty shop. I watched, and they taught me. I would do the big boy haircut. That is how I got started. One day a mother brought her little boy into the shop. He was so scared. He was crying while Peggy was trying to cut it. I went over and started talking to him. 'What is wrong? Are you ok sweetie?' I took his hand and said, 'I am Sally what is your name?' He stopped crying and looked up at me. I smiled at him, 'what is your name?' He just looked at me with a little smile. 'I bet your name is mmmm let me think. I know what it is it's "Good looking" that's your name.' 'No,' he said with a little giggle. 'That is your name I can see it written all over your face.' 'My name is Tommy' he said proudly. 'Are you sure?' I asked him 'Because I think I see good looking all over your face.' I turned the chair, so he could see himself. 'See, I told you it is all over your face and I don't think you can wipe that off.' He looked at his face in the mirror. 'No, it's not' he giggled."

"Peggy stepped in to start cutting his hair. The little boy shouted, 'Mommy I want Sally to do it.' Peggy shrugged her shoulders at me and handed me the scissors. That was my first official big boy cut." Jova sat there. The tension in him went away quickly as she talked. Her touch was soft. Her fingers stroked his hair more like a caress. He never felt like this when old Tilt Johnson cut his hair down at the old barbershop. When his hair was done, she began cutting on his beard. He had thought to stop her but chose to just be quiet. She was biting her lip and smiling while she continued talking. "I remember the little boys on Sunday's. They would have their big boy haircuts. They would be dressed in their Sunday best sitting in the church, they were so sharp, even shiny black shoes. Parents tried to keep them clean until the end of mass. Oh, and the little girls were so precious. In their little white dresses, some also had the white stockings, oh and the little white shoes with silver buckles on them." They were like dolls in the toy store.

"Once mass was over, they would tear off to the

playground on the side of the church. Some parents dragged their kids' home. Their kids weren't getting dirty in the good clothes at all. Then there were the parents that kept yelling not to get dirty. Then the parents who either gave up or just gave in. Just let the kids play. The men would huddle up and would catch up about the news or sports. The ladies would gossip about the scandals in the rag magazines. Some would talk about recipes they had tried. Some were good and some were great failures. They discussed kid's teachers and about the schools. All the while the kids were running, swinging and climbing. There was nothing like playing after church. We would play on the playground all the time. But to do it when you were supposed to stay clean or in your good clothes, that was like being allowed to do something wrong and not getting in trouble. I guess like a forbidden fruit thing."

She applied shaving cream to his face. He thought about Sally. The picture of the sweet girl. Who was taken captive? The frightened girl strapped to that table with so much fear in her eyes. The beautiful girl who appeared in my kitchen last night. The beautiful girl with soft hands cutting my hair. The beautiful girl rubbing his cheek.

"You are all done, Sweetie, smooth as a babies patootie." She smiled at him. He was stuck in the moment just gazing into her eyes. Maybe we should change your name to 'good looking' too," she said, as she bit her lip and dabbed his nose with her finger. She held the towel up to try to keep the hair from falling on the floor. His gaze followed her as she backed away with the towel. He cleared his throat and looked down at the floor. "Thank you" he said to her sincerely. "My pleasure, kind sir," she gleefully replied.

He slowly moved down the hallway. He just thought about how good he felt, his head was lighter with all that hair gone, and how good that food tasted, and his stomach was so full.

The hot water fell over him. As he washed, he felt all the scars. The good feeling started fading away. That nurse's face and her turning away. Then seeing her have to force herself not to look away later, when he knew she wanted too. Then excusing herself quickly. The happy feeling fell away with the water. An uneasy feeling came over him. He pictured other people fearing his face. Children pointing at him in fear.

He did realize that Sally never looked away. She was always smiling at me. That nurse's reaction kept coming back into his thoughts. He dried himself several times. He raised his hand to wipe the steam from the mirror, then chose not to. He entered his bedroom. With great astonishment, he looked around. The room looked like a bedroom. Sally's voice came from the hallway. "Just put your undies on for now. I got to put this ointment on you." A filling of shyness came over him.

Nervously he said, "That's ok I, I, I will do it." He stuttered. "Nonsense!" she replied. He quickly put on his underwear. "Ok, I'm coming in," she announced. He stood in the middle of the room with his eyes closed tightly, as if his eyes closed kept her from seeing him. She tried to make him not feel self-conscious by saying, "I bet you feel better being all clean now. I love how a hot shower it makes me feel great, all clean and ready to go out into the world."

She rubbed the ointment on his legs. At first, one cut at a time but with so many cuts she just ended up rubbing it on him like a lotion, then she did his sides and arms. She patted his belly "We need to get some meat on you. Don't worry I'll fatten you up like a Christmas turkey.

I'll have to put you on a diet in no time." She snorted a little when she laughed. He noticed she was tiptoeing to do his face. He got down on his knees and said in a quiet voice "Is this better?" She replied in a soft voice "Yes, better." She caressed his cheek for a small moment and said, "There is the handsome man who saved me." Her hand came away slowly. She was at a loss for words. She nervously cleared her throat and said, Umm, umm put a white t-shirt on. You are all shiny like one of those wrestlers now.

WOOF, WOOF, came from the front door. Jova smiled at her "It must be time for my walk." She bit her lip and dabbed his nose with her finger. "Well, get dressed, then you show off," as she sauntered away out of the room. He put on his police sweatsuit and appeared from the bedroom.

She was on the porch rubbing Dudes side talking to him. "He's a good boy, yes," she is talking with an excited childlike voice. His tail was wagging almost fast, which was super fast for The Dude. Jova slowly limped down the stairs. Dude took up the lead and stayed a few steps ahead. He would take a sniff, look around. Sometimes he would stop and look off into the trees and bushes.

Sally walked beside Jova and she marveled at the scenery. "Those wildflowers smell wonderful. Oh, look at that a blue butterfly. Ah, a hummingbird" she quietly pointed. "It is so small his wings don't stop at all, do they?" Jova whispered to her "That's a girl hummingbird." She looked at him how can you tell?" He answered, "My grandma told me. The boys have a ring around their neck and the girls don't." Sally whispered back "Aren't you the naturalist." He shook off the comment and said, "Nah I just remembered that. Grandma loved watching the birds, the trees waving in the breeze, the birds singing."

Jova pointed "There's a squirrel up in the trees - look at how fast he goes. He's sideways on a tree running faster than I can run in a straight line down a hill." Dude stops and watches the squirrel, then moves along. Sally watched Dude and said, "He is like a scout on an African safari, checking everything out for you." Jova smiled and said, "When he is on the job, he is on the job." After the second lap Dude climbed on to the porch and flopped down facing the field. "I think someone is on break. Sally jovially pointed out. "Do you have any request for lunch?" Jova looked up at the blue sky while soaking in the warmth of the sun. He said, "I think that you have a proven track record and will outdo any thought I have. So, I shall leave it in your more than capable hands." Sally looked down and smiled. They walked a little more and Jova spoke up "Ok, I have had enough." He limped up the steps to the house and made it on to the couch and he sat down. Sally shut the door. She came over to him and felt his head and said with concern, "You are still a bit on the warm side." She grabbed some water and a couple more pills. "Take these." He leaned forward and took them from her.

She watched him for a minute. He was fast asleep just sitting there. She wandered around the room. The house seemed to have stopped in time. Old pictures hung on the wall. A young Jova in his graduation gown. Then a picture of him in his police uniform was the newest picture. An old painting of St. Andrew on the saltire cross with Russian words across the bottom. A couple of snapshots of a young boy on an old farm tractor. An older man in bib overalls and a baseball cap behind standing behind him. It must be Jova and his grandpa.

There was an old cabinet style hi-fi with lace doilies, with a figure of St. Andrew on display. Some albums lay across the top of the hi-fi. There was Rachmaninoff, Tchaikovsky, Rimsky-Korsakov and Lawrence Welk. Two candles set in front of a picture of a young couple. Little knickknacks of angels watched over the house. The kitchen was old except for the refrigerator, stove and the coffee maker, which were still ten years old at least.

She moved to the bedrooms. One door opened to a sewing room, with an old black cast iron Singer sewing machine, and a large table to lay out fabrics and patterns. There were shelves holding different fabrics and scraps all stored for future use. Everything was dusty but looked ready to go. She opened another door and found a room with moving boxes stacked in it. Several boxes were empty with clothes marked on them.

The last bedroom had a canopy bed and wooden dressers that looked to be handmade. The bed looked handmade, too. Nearby, was a free-standing mirror. Two nightstands were on either side of the bed. A pile of books lay on each one, with reading glasses laid out on the top book. The bed was made up with a quilt covering the bed. She recognized some of the fabric from the sewing room.

She could just picture the old couple up in the bed, reading to each other a funny part or something interesting in the book. Oh, and a little Jova would be sitting in the middle while Grandma read a fairy tale to him or Grandpa looking over his homework, patting him on the back for a good report card. Old perfume bottles with an atomizer were on the dresser and a little dish with coins in it.

Later that evening the jingle, jingle sound rang through the house as Sally stirred her coffee. Jova stood up and made his way to the coffee pot. Sally watched him as he limped across the floor. He took a gulp of coffee. She reached over and felt his head. You are still warm. A growl came from Jova's stomach. Woof, woof, came from the front door. Sally opened the front door.

Dude stood at the door opening and took a big sniff and slowly strolled in. Sally smiled since he was not in a hurry at all. Jova filled his bowl. Dude flopped down paws on either side of the bowl. Jova sat down at the table, sipping the coffee.

CHAPTER 3

PRINCESS SALLY AND THE PALE PRINCE

Sally asked "Well, what would you like for dinner?" "That chicken from last night would be great." She began getting containers from the refrigerator. "It's a shame you don't have a magic box here." Jova looked puzzled. She clarified "I'm sorry a microwave." "I got one, it's in the back room. Hang on I'll get it." He moved the stacks of boxes around. There it was at the bottom of the pile. He set it down on the kitchen counter and plugged it in and sat back down.

Sally heated up the food and served it up while talking. "My father would read me bedtime stories when I was a young one. Every once in awhile, he would just make one up. That's when he got excited about the story."

"He told me this one several times. Once upon a time, there was a beautiful princess. Her name was Princess Sally. She was so beautiful that when she walked into the garden, the flowers would bloom just to be close to her. Wherever she walked things grew. The crops grew better. The grass was greener. The people were all so happy in the kingdom. Now there was a dark kingdom too - far away, but not too far away. The king was sad, as his wife had died a long time ago. He was pale, and the kingdom was grey. The people of the kingdom were all sickly and sad. One day the king called the young prince in. He was so pale and sad looking too. 'Yes, father, you sent for me?' 'Son, I have heard of a beautiful princess in a faraway land. She has been known to change the ground just by walking on it. Our kingdom is withering away so you must go court her. I soon will pass and follow your mother to Gods land above. You will need a queen for your kingdom. Someone to show you love and happiness.' The prince spoke powerfully, 'I will demand her hand. If they do not agree I shall take her by force.' The king grabbed him and said, 'Stop and listen. Son, I have taught you many things, but this is the most important. Love cannot be forced it must be given. So be off and try your best and be gentle with love.' The prince galloped along on his horse. He entered the kingdom. He just stopped in amazement. He was looking at all the colors - they were so bright and plentiful. He was brought before the king. He bowed in respect to the King and said, 'I have come for your daughter's hand sire.' The king stared at him and said in a bold voice, 'My daughter, the princess, is my treasure. What do you offer for her hand?' 'I will soon be king of my kingdom and I wish her to be my queen.' The king stared at him. 'That is not enough. I will only take two things for her and you must tell me what they are, before I will consider you for a son.' The prince held his mouth clenched. The king thought for a moment. 'I will give you some time to think. So, for now, be my guest while you think.' The prince was frustrated and was led away. The prince came to a large glass paned door that led to the garden. The flowers were so colorful. He was stunned and frozen staring out at everything. Then the beautiful Princess Sally came into view. She smiled at him and waved. Closer and closer she came. His chest began to hurt. He felt sick. Her beauty was too much for him to absorb all at once. The door opened, and she was right there. She reached out for his hand. His hand touched hers and he passed out and fell to the floor. She knelt beside him and held his head in her lap. His eyes opened 'Oh fair princess, please don't leave my side until I have died.' She stroked his hair. She caressed his cheek with her hand. She smiled 'I will not leave you, my prince.' Then something strange began to happen. His skin began to show color. His frown became a smile. His eyes slowly opened. She smiled at him. He felt so odd, but he was feeling better, as she stroked his cheek. Her eyes closed, and she slumped over him. He jumped to his feet, picked her up and he carried her to her bed. He yelled out to send for the doctors of the Kingdom. She just lay there in a deep, deep sleep motionless. The prince was frantic 'What can be done?' he pleaded. Finally, a maid-servant pulled him away. 'Sir, the only person that can save her is the wizard of the forest.' The prince galloped fast to the forest. He was told to go to a cave, where he boldly stomped in shouting, 'Wizard, wizard I must have your help.' The wizard appeared from the shadows. 'What may I help you with?' said the wizard. The prince told the wizard of the Princess's demise.

'You need Aphrodite's magic box.' The prince said, 'Well come now Wizard, with the magic box, we must waste no time.' The wizard said in a mysterious tone 'Prince, only you can work the box.' The wizard said, 'You must bake a small piece of bread in it and then feed it to her.' The prince looked at the box and said, 'This is made of wood it will burn up in the fire.' The wizard stopped him 'Oh no, no not a fire by wood, nor coal, nor oil shall make this box work for it is a magic box. That is all I can tell you.' The prince stormed away on his horse clutching the box to his chest. He made it back to the palace and then to the kitchen. He frantically mixed up some bread dough. He placed it in the box, but no magic. He raced to her bedside. He knelt beside her clutching the box to his chest with one hand and softly grasping her hand with his other. He began to cry 'Please, please don't leave me, fair princess.' Tears fell from his face. Some landed on the box. It began to glow so bright as if a piece of the sun were in it. He opened the box - a small piece of bread had baked in it. He tore off a piece and placed it in her mouth. 'Please, please come back to me my beautiful Princess.' Her lips began to move, and her eyes slowly opened. The prince's head was resting on her hand. 'Raise your head prince.' His head rose with tears in his eyes. 'Why do you weep prince?' she asked in a soft voice. A big grin came from him and he said, 'I could not bear the thought of not seeing you again.' She smiled and said, 'Then I must live.' Later the prince knelt before the king. 'Oh, king, I ask once again may I have your daughter's hand?' The king replied 'Well, what do you have to offer?' The prince took a deep breath, 'I have only my love and life to offer.' The king stared down at him, then over to his daughter. He grinned, and she nodded her head 'yes'. The king spoke loud and bold, 'You have my blessing.' The prince and princess rode to the far-off kingdom. As they entered the kingdom, flowers began to bloom, people began to smile, birds sang songs and they all lived happily ever after. The end. I must have made him tell that story for six months straight," She said.

She placed the plate in front of him. She backed away to the counter. She said, "Well dig in." He asked, "Won't you eat with me?" She bashfully answered, "No, no go ahead I'm fine." Her stomach growled loudly. He put on a determined face and crossed his arms, so she made a plate quickly and sat down. She took a bite defiantly. He unfolded his arms proudly and took a bite. He smiled and asked, "Do you know how great this food is? I would only have lasted a couple more minutes." She grinned and said, "I know, I let you win." Then she stuck her tongue out at him.

She began talking again. "My father would sometimes help me with my homework. He would start out good and then things would seem to trail off out of control. Once he was telling me about dinosaurs. The Brontosaurs, Stegosaurs, Triceratops and the T-rex. Then he would go off into why T-Rex's can't eat peanut butter. First off, they don't have spoons. Second, if they get a big mouthful it gets stuck to the roof of their mouths. Then they walk around smacking their lips, trying to get it off. Third, they can't open the jars, because they don't have thumbs. Finally, their moms get mad when they leave peanut butter fingerprints all over the kitchen. He would stomp around smacking his lips imitating a T-rex. saying do you have any peanut butter?' and growl and roar? I would giggle so much I would wet myself. One day I was in school and the class was talking about dinosaurs. I just started giggling. The teacher asked me what was so funny about dinosaurs? I, of course, answered 'They can't eat peanut butter.' My dad had to go in for a teacher's meeting. He told them the story. I think they thought he was short bus special." She was putting the dishes away and turned with a smile and a tear.

Jova nervously stood up and went to her. She hugged him tightly, "I miss him so much." Jova rubbed her back and in a low voice said, "It's okay, it's okay." Her ear was against his chest and she could feel the vibration as he talked. The room went quiet as they held each other. She took a big sniffle and he handed her a napkin. She wiped her eyes and said, "Look at me crying like a little schoolgirl with a skinned knee." She hugged him thank you. He rubbed her back and the room was silent once more. He said in a low tone, "I have peanut butter if you want some." She snorted out in laughter.

Dude stood up and was staring at them. Sniffing at them, he nudged Sally with his nose. She leaned over and rubbed his sides and head and asked, "Are you ready to go, are you ready to go outside?" She said it so excitedly Dude even perked up, wagging his tail and shaking his head. She let him out.

She asked Jova "Come on and sit on the swing for a moment with me." Jova limped out to the porch swing. It was a large swing Big enough for two to sit without touching if they chose too. He moved awkwardly to sit down close to the armrest. The swing gently rocked back and forth.

She began speaking calmly, "My mother died four years ago. Then my father died a year later." Her hand reached over and grasped his. "Jova I'm so scared I can't sleep. When I try to sleep, I feel like I am trapped. A heavy weight falls over me and I feel like I can't move. I can barely breathe. I'm just trapped all alone in nothingness. I constantly keep moving. If I stop, that feeling comes over me and it is so, so horrible." Her hand grasped his tighter and tighter and her voice grew more frantic. Tears streamed down her cheeks. He put his arm around her and pulled her in close. She continued, "I miss my parents so much. I felt so safe with them and now this happens. I keep pretending I'm ok. They say time heals all things and I pray and pray, but when I stop for a moment, that feeling comes over me and I get so scared." She shuttered under his arm, as his hand rubbed, up and down her arm. Her head leaned into his side, she grew quiet, with a sniffle here and there. He just sat there rubbing her arm. Her grasp slowly went soft. She had fallen into a deep sleep.

They sat there for a while just gingerly swinging. The night air was getting cool. He went back and forth in his mind, whether or not to pick her up or just sit there and let her rest. He committed to the thought of carrying her to the bedroom and hoped she would stay asleep. He grasped her up in his arms. Gently he limped through the house, softly placed her on the bed and pulled the blanket up to her chin. Dude came in and sniffed at her and flopped down beside the foot of the bed. Jova with empathy stood there gazing at her. He looked at dude lying there. Jova pulled a chair over close to the bed. He sat down quietly to watch over her.

The next day came it was late afternoon. Jova was eating the leftovers. He went back to the bedroom. She was still sleeping. He began walking his laps in the yard and he thought all about Sally and he worried. Should he call a doctor or the shrink or just let her sleep. He walked eight laps without realizing it. Visions of Sally filled his thoughts. He thought of the way she would, bite her lip and then smile, her dabbing his nose, her caressing his face and putting that ointment on him, playfully sticking her tongue out at him. He sat in the chair watching over her. Dude was lying at her side too.

The next morning, Jova was cooking in the kitchen. He sat down at the table and was drinking his coffee. A disheveled look of beauty appeared and stood at the edge of the kitchen, rubbing her eyes. A big smile came over Jova "Good morning sleepy head." She gave a pouty smile and said, "Good morning" in a quiet tone.

Jova rose to greet her as she sat down at the table. He poured her a cup of coffee and asked, "Cream and sugar, right?" She grinned a yes. He asked, "Are you hungry?" She said, "I am famished." He grabbed a bowl and filled it with oatmeal and placed it down in front of her, with a spoon stuck in it.

He set it down as he spoke. "It's my own concoction. It's oatmeal with crunchy granola raisin bran mixed in." She took a bite and chewed slowly. She began nodding her head and said, "This is pretty good." He was glad she liked it.

She asked how he come up with this concoction. He wiped his mouth with a napkin. "Well, one day I wanted to have cereal but I was out of milk. So, I made some oatmeal. I took one bite and I just wanted the cereal more than ever. So, in my breakfast desperation, I just dumped the box of cereal on top of the oatmeal. To my surprise, it tasted good."

"How do you feel?" he asked with concern. She smiled and replied, "Much better, that was all I needed. Just one good night of sleep." She smiled at him and said, "Wow, your whiskers grow fast!" She looked puzzled at him. "That's a lot of growth in a day. You must have to shave twice a day. Some men are like that though strangely enough, they're usually bald. It's kind of ironic, I guess." Jova smiled as she talked. "Then some men are bald because they choose to. Poor guys that are just plum depressed about the hair on their head falling out. Then comes in a guy with a full head of hair and says take it all off. I want the bald look. I do remember one fellow - he had a little money to him. He went off to one of those hair plugs places. They take the hair from areas of the head where it is still growing and place them in the bald spot. After all that stuff, he went through, it fell out anyway. Then he had craters all over his head. If he would have just left it alone, he would have a smooth head at least. I guess some people try to hang on to things as long as they can. You have good hair I doubt you will ever have a balding problem. Based on your granddad's picture, your family has good genetic hair. That is a big plus in your favor. I do believe some skip a generation. So, I guess nothing is one hundred percent. One minute you got all your hair and the next it's all falling out."

"One minute you're going to your car and some maniac grabs you." She took a deep breath and began tearing up. She covered her mouth with a shuddering hand. He came to her side and knelt beside her. She reached out and grasped him hard. Her head fell on to his shoulder. Her tears were flowing strong. He rubbed her back and whispered in her ear, "Let it all out you're safe, let it out, you're safe let it out." She hugged him so hard it almost took his breath away. She held him for what seemed to be a whole day. She went limp in his arms. He wasn't sure what to do again. He slowly leaned her back and her eyes were closed. She had fallen asleep in his arms. He picked her up and carried her to the bedroom. He gingerly placed her on the bed. Dude followed behind watching every move. Jova pulled the blanket up to her chin again. As Jova stepped back gazing at her. Dude came alongside the bed his nose up and sniffing at her. He looked at Jova and he lay down beside the bed. Jova sat down in the chair beside the bed, and watched her as she slept, wondering if he should he call someone to help her?

When he was on the job, there was a list of numbers to hand out to victims of various incidents, and of course, you can send them to the hospital. A social worker would point them in whatever direction of help that was available. This was the first time he saw what weeks after the trauma was like. They would always stress, if possible make sure they have someone to go home to, family or friends.

He pondered over the many faces he had seen over his career. Faces in pain, shock, loss, and bewilderment. What they all went through after the event, when everyone left, and the flashing lights had disappeared into the distance. Some were left all alone. Those thoughts were heavy on him for a while, as he gazed upon her sleeping so soundly.

He got up and slowly moved out of the room and limped out to the front porch. He rubbed his leg as to give it a good massage. He began walking around his yard as he thought of Sally and the many stories she told. She talked so fast. He thought of her in wondrous ways, like when she bites her lip on a pause. She surely can cook very well. He never felt so good as when she cut his hair. Her touch was so soft as she stroked his hair, running her fingers through it so gently. She was so lovely, she was the princess in that story. When she rubbed the ointment on him, he giggled to himself. Wow, if he wasn't still in pain from the wounds, she would have known how he felt about her.

He made 12 laps and with his mind so busy, his pain was minor, and the laps went fast. He sat down on the porch swing. As he sat quietly his eyes slowly closed, his thoughts of her faded and that nurse's reaction replayed over and over. He dwelled on people's reaction to his appearance. His thoughts began to exaggerate in his mind's eye. People's reaction grew worse and worse. He began to feel his stomach tighten. Despair fell upon him.

CHAPTER 4

JANIE AND WILLIAM

The day before, back in the city, in a seedy bar in a rough part of the city, men were flying through the air and not by the greatest of ease and not by their choice. A mammoth of a man flung the so-called manly men about like rag dolls.

Four police officers entered the building. Six men with broken pool sticks surrounded the mammoth man all - moving side to side. None wanted to move on him but, all the adrenaline and testosterone was flowing, along with blood and spilled beer. The officers lined up, side by side. The lead officer loudly and sternly yelled "EVERYONE FREEZE!!! STOP FIGHTING AND DROP YOUR WEAPONS... NOW!!!!!!"

The mammoth man smirked but held his ground. He made no gesture either way, whether he was done and complying or ready to continue fighting. The officers began gripping their nightsticks in anticipation of taking on the giant. The smallest officer took a step forward. She stared at the man and spoke. "I will take him. You guys take the rest of them."

The other officers gulped down their nervousness. The men that had him surrounded, looked back at her and then at him with their mouths hanging open in disbelief at her confidence. She placed her night-stick in her belt. Her hands were empty of weapons. She approached him. The circle of men parted. Silence gripped the place. Drips of spilled beer seem to be the only sound as everyone watched the one officer move towards the mammoth man.

His eyes followed her as she moved closer and closer until she stood in front of him. The size difference was amazing - he had almost 2 feet on her and 250lbs of muscle. She spoke firmly and asked, "Do you want to do this the hard way or the easy way?" He looked down at her and said, "Your choice officer." She looked up at him and took a deep breath and said, "It's been a long day I would prefer the easy way. So, get your big ass over here and put your hands behind your back." He did as she instructed without complaint or pause. He winced a little as he put his hands behind his back.

She spoke, "Has your shoulder been bothering you?" "Yes, he said. She looked up at him and said, "I will cuff you in the front instead." He replied, "Thank you, officer." "You're welcome" she answered with complete control of the situation. He placed his hands in front and she clipped the cuffs on him, and he bowed his head down like a little boy with the look of shame on his face.

The place was dead silent mouths still gaping open as she led him out. She spoke, "You will be coming with me to the station." He answered her with complete respect. "Sure, anything you need officer," he replied. As she walked him out, she talked to him. "They didn't use their good manners with you, did they?" He looked at the floor as they walked, and said, "No, they were very impolite to me."

She opened the door to allow him to exit the establishment and said with stern disappointment, "William, I have told you before - not everyone was raised with proper manners." He replied, "I know, but saying please, thank you, excuse me and you're welcome. I don't think that is asking too much and I stopped concerning myself with people's nonuse of; yes sir, no sir and yes mam, no ma'am and eating with the right cutlery stuff. I really don't expect you are welcome either."

"But when some guy starts yelling at me 'get the hell out of my way or I am going to piss in your drink.', I get a little irritated and then his friends say they are going to piss in my drink too. So, I stood up to correct them in their communication skills. I explained to them what they were doing was all wrong. They just stood there looking at me. They seemed to be making funny faces at me, but no one spoke. No one replied and they didn't excuse themselves from the conversation they just stood there staring at me. Well, you saw them. "She rubbed his arm reassuringly and just said, "William. "He looked at her and replied I know I'm sorry."

More police showed up as they were talking. All were jumping out of their vehicles quickly to assist. They all looked in amazement as they watched her leading him out to her police car. Again, the size difference between the officer and the man and her confidence with her head held high in complete control of him was astonishing to the onlookers.

William got a big smile on his face and asked "Hey, can we stop off at that vegan burger joint please, please, with sugar on top, please?" She looked at him and paused for a moment. She agreed "That does sound good. I do love their fries too, oh and a brownie, mmmm." She smiled at him and replied "That sounds like a wonderful idea. Thank you for inviting me, kind sir." He grinned, "You are most graciously welcome, kind lady." He was as excited as a little kid.

She yelled over to the other policemen. "Hey, I'm going to take a dinner break on the way to the station. I'll be about an hour." One of the policemen spoke up very puzzled, "Ok ..." They all looked at each other and then moved toward the front door of the bar to assist the other officers. As the men came out in handcuffs, they all had an odd look about them.

As they drove, William spoke, "You remember Karen? She came back yesterday. She brought the baby in. The baby is so beautiful. She was holding my finger and smiling. I'm going to start Karen up on a low impact work out program next week. She'll be back in shape in no time."

He leaned forward and said, "You know most wonderful and lovely, Officer Janie Mazerick, I think you would be so wonderful at holding a baby of your very own." "Slow down, "Mom!!!" she said quickly and sarcastically. She looked at him through the rearview mirror. He smiled at her and playfully said, "Come on, you know I get giddy around babies. I still think we would make beautiful children." She looked at him, blushing, through the rear-view mirror and answered, "Oh, you think everyone is beautiful." He smiled and said, "This is true, but I think you're the most wonderful and truly lovely woman I have ever met. If you will take me back, I will never point out your animal unfriendly shoes and I will almost hold out for at least 6 ballroom dance lessons." She blushed and looked at him again through the mirror. She spoke in a stern voice, "I'll agree to 3 with a right to refuse or renew 3 more. No arguments and I'm free to refuse with no explanation." He grinned from ear to ear.

"This is the fourth happiest day of my life." She looked at him puzzled and said, "FOURTH?" He leaned forward and spoke, "The happiest will be when you agree to marry me. The second will be when we have our first child. The third will be when we have our second child. The fifth will be our third child. The sixth will be---" he mumbled something unclear. "What? What was that last thing?" she asked. He said clearly, "When you give up leather shoes." She pointed at him in the mirror. He spoke loudly and jovially, "The sixth happiest will be our fourth child or when our first child graduate's college." She smiled and said, "The college one, I like that."

He leaned back with a large smile and self-assuredly said, "Ok, I think I'm going to have a whole big bunch of happy days coming the next fifty years." She also had a big smile too.

She changed her tone and asked, "Oh, and by the way would you help an old friend of mine? He's coming back from some injuries and needs a little help. He wants to train alone at home, but I think he is a little self-conscious. He got cut up badly on his last case." He replied, "If it is your wish, I would be happy to. So, let it be written, so let it be done." She smiled at him and said, "Good we will head out early tomorrow."

The next day they arrived at Jova's house. The car crept slowly up as it came up the dirt driveway. Jova rose from the porch swing to greet them, and he made his way down the steps. Janie hugged him and said, "It's damn good to see you, Jova. This is my boyfriend William. He's going to get you back in shape." Jova looked up at him and said, "Good morning William. "William looked at him sternly at first, then burst out with a big smile and shook his hand "It's an honor to meet you, sir. Janie told me about you, and I would be honored to help you." Jova was humble and replied with "Well thank you." He seemed to be a little puzzled by William's response.

Janie smiled at Jova and said, "I will explain it later, but where is the bathroom?" Jova smiled and answered, "Down the hallway." William spoke up, "Alrighty then let us get started. I need you to be honest with me when I ask you how you feel. Have you been doing any kind of exercise?" Jova replied "I have been trying to get walks in regularly every day, a little more each day. I just did 12 laps around my yard about an hour ago." William responded, "Excellent, excellent, you are actually trying already. That is fantastic, I'll have you in fighting shape in no time. Let us get you stretched out and evaluate your range of motion."

Janie walked past the bedroom and Dude watched her every move. She continued to the bathroom. On her way back looked in to see a covered Sally lying asleep in the bed with Dude watching over her faithfully. She stepped out on the porch to see Jova's extremities being pushed and pulled in all sorts of directions and some did not seem possible.

She had a big grin as she watched. Jova made many new facial expressions while William was working on him. William said, "Go get some shorts on and I will set up the massage table out here." William took Jova's hand and pulled him to his feet.

As Jova opened the door. Janie whispered, "Who's in the bed?" Jova answered, "Sally Ann." She stopped him and quietly said with a serious tone, "You mean the victim?" You know that's taking advantage." He cut her off saying, "I have not done anything. She showed up several days ago and I did not initiate this. She showed up on her own and made me some dinner to thank me. I told her it was not necessary and thanks. She would not take no for an answer. I think she is all alone and needed to be around someone. She needed someone to talk to. I have to admit it's not hurting me for her to be here. I tell you; she surely brightened my life up the past several days." He said with conviction, "Besides my own feelings, she has a lot of stuff under the surface she needs to get through and I'm no shrink, but I sure can see she needs some kind of help. If not, just some time to deal with what just happened. She has been asleep for almost 3 days straight. That's got to be good for something. Almost everything that has ever been wrong with me some doctor has said get plenty of rest."

Janie tried to think of a counter-argument but just sighed and said "Ok. You know in our training they teach us that a victim can be in a very delicate state." Jova replied, "Yes and I concur, so should I just close my door to her?" Janie was staring at him, she paused, trying to compose her thoughts. Jova added, "Janie how many car accident victims have we just held their hands until they calmed down?"

William interrupted, "Come on, let's get a move on, you two can talk later. I need him on the table. I don't want to lose this beautiful day." Jova was in and out of the house quickly. He opened the door wearing old shorts and a tee shirt. William barked out, "Lose the shirt and get up on the table." In just his shorts, he climbed on to the table face down.

As he walked down the steps with all his scars exposed, Janie did not react, but she realized how much of a toll Jova took on this case. William did not react to the scars. He was more like a doctor, examining with a clinical eye and feeling his body for a more thorough examination.

He began the massage, Janie yelled down with a

laugh, "Don't expect a happy ending. She sat down on the steps and watched as William worked on him. Jova's face went from pleasure to pain many times. Janie grinned at the expressions and sometimes laughed.

Jova mumbled to her, "I see you are having a good time at my expense." She laughed. "I can't help it. It's not like, the massage parlors we use to bust downtown is it?" He smiled, "No it's not." His face contorted and his voice grunted out the words as he spoke. William rubbed him for a good hour. He asked, "How do you feel now?" Jova with his eyes closed, "Very relaxed." William happily said, "Excellent, now the fun begins."

William got a big smile on his face and barked out, "Ok, up on your feet. Let's get started," as he pulled a plastic drink container out of his gym bag. He handed it to Jova and said, "Here, drink this straight down." It was a homemade concoction of some sort. William smiled with great confidence "It will make a human being strong. You might even grow an inch today before we are done." Janie said, "Jova, just drink it fast don't think about it," Janie giggled. Jova looked back at her for reassurance. She nodded her head and smiled as she said, "Really fast, and don't stop until you are done." He finally just tilted it up and drank it down. He finished with a horrified face, "That tasted like grass with mud mixed in." William laughed, "It is! No, I'm just kidding you. It is seaweed, vitamins and soy protein powder mix and some other herbs. It's even got some fiber and bran in there too. So, don't be surprised, later tonight, if you feel the need to go to the bathroom.

Also, I would not take a chance if you feel the urge to go."

William said with glee "Ok, what will we make your safe word?" William placed his forefinger on his lips, and he thought for a minute and announced, "Mmmmm, 'Jesus loves me'. That is a good safe word - I like it." Jova looked very puzzled at him and at Janie. Jova asked,"A safe word? Why would we need a safe-word?" Without answering, William ordered Jova all over the yard and to do various stretches and exercises.

Janie sat on the porch swing smiling, as off in the distance she kept hearing Jova saying "JESUS LOVES ME" and William would reply, "YES HE DOES"

The screen door opened, and Sally peered out. Janie looked over and smiled, "Good morning. I'm Janie, Jova's old partner. Come on out and have a seat." They sat for a while watching and talking. While off in the distance, you could hear, "JESUS LOVES ME" "YES HE DOES" But they never stopped.

Sally spoke up, "I did not know Jova was that openly religious type." Janie smiled and said, "He is now and I imagine the next couple of days he's going to talk to Jesus a lot. How about us girls go have a coffee in the house?" Sally said, "That sounds good and we can make them something to eat." Janie said, "I got some stuff in the car I'll be right in."

Sally looked concerned for Jova as she looked out in the yard. Janie came up the steps with a bag. She saw the concern in Sally's face. "Don't worry about them, they will be just fine." Sally looked puzzled and tilted her head sideways. "That does not seem natural to me." Beside Sally's leg, was Dude with his head tilted sideways also. Janie laughed, "They will be fine, just fine."

The girls went into the house. Dude plopped down to continue watching out in the yard, his head tilting to right to left and back again from time to time. Finally, he just placed his head down. Off in the distance, their voices still could be heard slightly "JESUS LOVES ME" "YES HE DOES"

Janie said, "If you don't mind, I'll make dinner. My boyfriend is vegan." Sally smiled and asked if that was contagious? Sally peered out the front door and asked, "How did he get so big eating lettuce?" Janie laughed and said' "He eats more than just salads." They both laughed. Sally said, "A man that big and he doesn't eat meat. That is amazing. All the vegans I have met have always seemed to look so malnourished. He certainly is an exception to the stereotype." Janie laughed and said, "He fits no stereotype, I can guarantee that. Sometimes it's downright odd." "In what way?" Sally asked, "Well, when I say these things, I don't mean them in a mean way." She thought for a moment. "I don't mean that it is bad, it's just nothing I'm used to." Sally was intrigued and said to Janie "Come on spill the beans."

Janie had a confused look while she tried to explain what she meant. "Of course, there is 'the vegan' thing. Then, he is super confident, but not in a bad way. You know what I mean, not like an asshole. You know the type - egotistical, pompous." Sally snorted out a laugh and said, "Oh yes." Janie continued on saying, "Things like he will wear clothes, I don't know, I guess that would lead one to wonder about his sexuality, and he thinks nothing about it. Neither does he care what people think either way. If he thinks it looks nice, and that is what he wants, he will wear it. "Sally asked, 'Well does he dress badly?" "No, that's the thing, he looks great. I guess I'm, more used to a traditional look of a man in blue jeans and a flannel shirt." Sally said, "Well that doesn't sound like a bad thing at all. Does he get angry or mistreat you or cheat?" Janie quickly answered, "Oh, heavens no, I just picked him up in a bar fight last night and he was fighting 6 guys. He wasn't even angry during that. During the whole fight, he never made a fist. He mostly just blocked their attacks and would tell them what they were doing wrong - why their fighting styles and moves were ineffective. He does seem to be overly consumed with people's manners though." Sally then asked, "In what way?" Janie, with apprehension, said, "Well, like table manners and how you treat people, those types of manners. Like saying you are welcome, when someone does something for you. If a waitress brings you a drink, you say thank you. If you bump someone you excuse yourself. Guys should be opening a door for women, and stuff like that." Sally sparked up and said, "That sounds great, too. A true gentleman." Janie agreed, "Yes, it is when you go to a place uptown, but he expects the same anywhere he goes. Last night he was in one of the worst parts of town still expecting thank you and you're welcome." Sally said, "Oh my, at least he is consistent." Sally asked, "He sounds like a man of conviction and integrity. Isn't that a good trait for a man to have?"

Janie ponders her thoughts and starts to reply and stops and starts again Her eyes get big and she says "CRAP! I just realized something about myself. I am so used to men/people that have such low character. That low character has become the normal standard for me." Janie had to let that sink in for a time with an amazed and disgusted look about her.

Sally thought she should keep her talking and asked, "How does he treat you?" Janie broke from her bad thoughts and smiled and answered, "He treats me great - I have never met a gentler and more caring man in my life. He is so sugary sweet, sometimes it's a little embarrassing. He does not run from any kind of commitment talk. Shoot, he is talking about having 4 kids with me and he wants to take ballroom dancing lessons for the wedding. He thinks that it would be fun whether we get married or not."

Sally said, "That sounds so sweet." Sally grinned with astonishment, "Well, he sounds perfect." Janie replied with a big smile, "That's the problem - there is no problem. I can't find a bad thing about him. He is like no other man I have ever met. He has no vices - he barely drinks. He might drink once a month and when he does, he really gets lovey-dovey." Sally says with a suggestive tone "Oh my." Sally covers her mouth with her hands and snorts out a laugh. They both giggle for a while.

Janie continues, "He does charity work. He owns two gyms. I have never heard him say a bad word towards anyone. He is so positive about everything and everyone. That's something I am surely not used too, especially with all the ugly things I see on my job.

Sally looked at her and asked, "Do you love him? I mean love him. Does he make you quiver? Do you feel safe around him? Do you trust him? Could you imagine a better man than him?" Janie answered with seriousness, "Yes, yes, yes, yes, and no." Janie blushed a little. Her eyes got watery. Sally handed her a tissue, "Sweetie, just let him love you and let go, and love him back." Sally rubbed Janie's back and said, "Sometimes we look at them through such a magnifying glass, we miss the truth that is right in front of us. You keep looking for something wrong in him. Now the fact you can't find anything becomes the flaw. You are a cop, you can see beneath the surface. So, you can figure out what is really going on. What is below the surface of William?" Janie thought for a moment. She got a big smile and said, "He is a big teddy bear who is just warm, and soft and he does have a flaw. He keeps bothering me about my shoes!" Sally looked puzzled and said, "Your shoes? He is not one of those shoe fetish guys, is he?" Janie laughed, "No, no he is a vegan. He doesn't like to see anything that is made from animal parts." Sally snorted and laughed, "Girl you are in trouble then." They both laughed. Janie's laugh turned into a very devious grin as she jumped up and ran out the front door straight towards William.

Jova heard her footsteps getting closer. He turned to see what was coming rather fast at them and William followed suit. Jova said "I think you have a delivery coming, I can't tell if it's good or bad, but good luck." Janie leaped on to William's chest and wrapped her arms around his big neck and planted a big kiss on him. He hugged her hard and kissed her back. She leaned her head just back far enough and said, "I love you, you, big silly teddy bear" and she kissed him again.

Jova smiled and quietly limped away thinking, 'I deserve a little breather, and this will be an ideal time to sit down, because I know Jesus loves me now.' Jova made it to the front door and Sally handed him a large glass of water and said, "Holy mackerel, those two are in quite the wrestling hold." Jova took a big drink of water looked back at them, and said, "I hope the match lasts long enough for me to rest up a couple of minutes. "Sally smiled and said, "You want a newspaper to read while you wait?" Jova said, "I think today's training torture is done I am going to try the hot shower." Sally watched him, with concern, as he limped back to the bathroom.

CHAPTER 5

WILLIAM'S STORY

That evening they sat down to eat. William said after his first bite, "This is delicious - you chefs really outdid yourselves mmmmmmm, beans and rice." Jova looked stiff as he tried to pick up his spoon. He moved slowly with many looks of discomfort and pain. William smiled and said to Jova, "Eat up, this will give you plenty of energy and help your body to recuperate. Tomorrow is coming fast." William was serious in his meaning, it was not a humorous dig or joke.

Sally watched Jova with great concern. She questioned, "William, are you sure he is ready for this much activity?" "Sure," he addressed her with great confidence, "I checked him over good. He will be fine I will have him in fighting condition in no time. I do this kind of rehab for the army, sometimes when they get wounded or suffer an injury. The docs tend to write them off from returning to duty too fast. But some want back in and will do whatever it takes. That's when they contact me. If they are willing, capable and really want to get back in proper shape I will push them the whole way. They must be willing and really want it or they just fade away and get used to a cane or wheelchair."

Sally said, "That is so sad. I thought the army would take care of its own." William wiped his mouth with a napkin and replied Oh, you misconstrued. When I say a person gets hurt, they get hurt in many ways, not only the physical but mentally too, they tend to get hurt worse. They no longer believe in being one hundred percent. They feel it is no longer possible to be what they were. I guess that is sometimes true. I try to explain to them this is a new starting point in their lives. Now is your chance to be reborn. To find out what the new you, are truly capable of. No more hiding in your past no more fooling yourself on your imaginary life. Everything is now gone, stripped away and taken from you - whatever way you want to look at it. Now you can go on a journey to find out what you, and only you, are now willing and capable to do and in no way is this journey easy, comfortable nor fair. That is why only so few truly take it. Their biggest obstacle is themselves. I am by no means a head doctor. I look at in a very simple way. The human body is capable of movements. I can make the body strong enough to move. Then the person must decide where he wants to take it. Some just take it to a chair. Some can run a marathon. I don't mean to sound judgmental or disparaging. I am only saying you can build the body up to what it is capable to do. I can make you strong enough to stand walk or run. If it is not capable, I will make it strong enough to make its best attempt to accomplish what they want to do."

"Take Jova here, he will be a fully capable policeman when I am done. He will be able to pass the police physical easily. He will, providing he wants to. I have no magic wand nor a magic pill. It all comes down to old fashion hard work. Now the methods I try to incorporate in the work out are geared towards a maximum result with least effort."

"Don't let the words 'least effort' stick in your head," He said with a big smile. "There will be a lot of sweat and energy excreted and from every part of your body. This is not, the old 'I wanna lose 10 lbs. for a special event' work out."

Janie laughed, "Ok, calm down with all that work talk at the dinner table." Jova looked tired just chewing. Sally spoke up, "I do find this very interesting. Sally asked, "You really have a deep thought on the new person arising from the ashes. It's like a reborn Christian or a butterfly emerging from a cocoon." William smiled with self-assurance and said, "That is it, you got it. I always looked at it more from a Buddhist thought of a reincarnation of yourself. That is the gist of it." Sally replied, "Like the old saying 'this is the first day of the rest of your life'."

Sally looked over to Jova whose eyes were closed, and he looked to be ready to fall face-first into his bowl. Sally stood up and grasped Jova's arm and said, "It is past your bedtime young man." Jova followed her to the bedroom, and he collapsed on his bed face first. She bit her lip as she pulled the cover to his shoulders. Dude nudged her hand as she gazed upon Jova. She reached down and rubbed his side and said, "Good boy, you want to go, you want to go out, don't you?" His tail wagged faster as her voice got higher. She let him out.

She started picking up dishes and to clean up after dinner. Janie asked, "Sally, how are you doing?" She smiled with her reply, "Oh just fine." It was a generic response with no meaning in it. Janie tried rephrasing "I mean since the incident." Sally just put on a not too believable look of sincerity and answered "Just peachy. The doctors released me, so, I am just fine."

Janie let it go and redirected towards Jova. "How has Jova been doing then?" Sally gladly answered, if only to change the subject. "He was a little slow-moving at first, but he has been getting some regular walks in. Certainly, nothing like William put him through today." She giggled a bit. William smiled and confidently said, "Don't worry, he will be just fine. Based on what I saw today, he has nothing to worry about." Sally asked William how he got started in this kind of work.

William took a deep breath and said, "I guess it started when I was in my teens. My father was in the military special forces and was the toughest and strongest man I ever knew. There was nothing that he could not do. No mountain too tall, or river too wide, he wouldn't attack it with his all, which made for a no-nonsense childhood for me. No excuses were allowed for anything, just results. I guess I had reached that age where I had had enough straight and narrow and wanted a little laziness, or just not to be on point every minute of the day. I came home from school one day and my mother was there in the living room hysterical and crying. One of my father's squad mates was there trying to keep her calm. I rushed to her side and held her hand. The man told me that my father had been hurt very badly on a mission and he was in the hospital. He got transported stateside 2 days later to the base hospital. My mother and I went to see him. He was able to put on a strong face for my mother's sake, but I saw something in his eyes for the first time ever. It was uncertainty and fear. He had lost one of his legs below the knee and one of his hands. I had taken his strength and abilities in our lives for granted. It cracked open a whole bunch of thoughts of doubt about my whole family's future."

"There were many trips back and forth to the hospital. It seemed like each time he drifted a little farther away from us. Then came the day the doctor sent him to the rehab facility. I saw them all. The dismembered, scarred, torn to shreds and patched back together with what was left. I saw the broken men. At first, I did not want to go back and face such sights, but I did not want my mother to face that all alone. I had to fill in for the old man until he was in better shape. As I began going to the rehab facility, I noticed something. I noticed what the will of a human is and what it could do and why it was so important."

"My father had given up and he had quit in his mind too. He was done. No more missions, no more to a lot of things he loved to do. They fit him with prosthetics and the time had come for him to answer the question - was he going to quit in front of his family or was he going to be the strongest, toughest man I ever knew and show us what true strength was? He faltered, and he bitched and complained. He was constantly frustrated.

"A man came up to him with two prosthetic legs, walking slowly but very well. He stopped my father when he was trying to use his new prosthetic hook with no success. He said in a stern military voice, 'Soldier stop all that bull shit and clear your head. Now focus on one small task. Grip the cup and raise it up 6 inches off the table and then put it down. Soldier, did you hear your mission orders? My father answered 'Yes sir' out of habit. "The man said, 'Then carry out your orders." My father started out fast and hard and the man shouted at him, 'Stop! Soldier, did I say there was a hard deadline on this mission? So, do it slowly and with care and achieve your objective and do not stop until it is done right and with quality.' My father made 3 attempts to grab the cup and raise it up. He then stopped, and he started working the hook moving it in every possible motion and watched it - how it reacted and operated - what his body had to do to make it work - and he mocked the motion and watched it closely. He slowly moved toward the cup. The hook began to open slowly, and he moved closer to the cup. With the cup within the pinchers, they slowly tightened and gripped the cup. He raised the cup slowly watching the cable tension. He had done it! He had accomplished what he had set out to do!

"That's when I saw the spark of life come back in my father's eyes. From that point on he was back in the game and I was right there with him. We both began learning how the body works. The range of motion and how to compensate for where it was lacking. He became so adept at working with prosthetics he began teaching other patients. He worked with them and helped motivate them for a positive outcome. I saw how accomplishing small achievements lead to accomplishing bigger achievements. Picking up a pencil could lead to a completed book. Standing on two prosthetic legs could lead to a father walking his daughter down the aisle and dancing with her at her wedding."

"The struggles and obstacles most people have are within themselves. The self-doubt and self-consciousness of how they look and how people view them, this can really affect their recovery too. It always struck me funny after seeing it so many times. The loved ones show up and they are just happy to see them alive. They hug and kiss them, and they all cry their eyes out. They are, at first, concerned with the son or husband's health and they always turn it around to themselves and how it affects them, though usually not in a bad way. For example, a mother began telling everyone how work will need to be done to the house, so her beautiful baby boy would not have any problems getting in her house for dinner. She added 'Well I guess that front flower garden I just finished will have to go.' She paused and kissed her son's forehead and said jovially, HECK WITH IT, I don't like gardening anyways. I just do it to piss off that busybody bitch neighbor 2 houses down the block.' She was not worried about his missing limb or his scars. The second she saw her baby was alive and well. She knew the road ahead was no big deal.

"They must overcome themselves and their inner roadblocks in order to face the ones out here in the real world. A setback one day could lead to success next week if you don't give up.

"So, you could say this work is in my blood and I was brought into the family business. I am very passionate about what I do too. So, don't worry about Jova. I will see to his wellbeing and although it looks harsh, it is what is best for his condition."

He turned to Janie, "Where do we sleep in this joint?" Sally spoke up, "Straight down the hallway there is a bedroom." He took a big drink from his cup and said, "I am ready for bed, myself." He bowed to Sally and Janie and said in a gentle regal tone, "Thank you for your lovely and pleasant company and conversation. I bid you a warm and soft goodnight. Sally curtseyed with a big grin, "We thank you kind gentleman."

Janie patted him on his back and said playfully, "Alright let's get a move on." She said goodnight to Sally and reached up to his shoulders, grabbing his traps and rubbing them as she pushed him down the hall. Williams' voice faded, but Sally heard him say, "I see some-ones putting in their 5-minute shoulder rub, expecting a 30-minute massage in return." Janie blurted out, "You bet your muscular ass I am, and including the feet." Sally laughed inside and was smiling, those two are something else.

CHAPTER 6

PAIN AND STIFFNESS

Early the next morning William's large hands tapped on Jova's door. "Let's get started Jova," William said with great enthusiasm. Jova pulled the covers over his face and said, "Crap I was hoping that was just a bad dream" As he tried to move, he gasped out a grown "oo-ooooooye ". His face was crooked with a look of pain. He got up and slowly walked to the kitchen table.

As his legs bent, ever so slowly, to sit down, his face showed many looks of discomfort throughout the whole process. William smiled, "Here is your breakfast," as he placed a large glass with a green thick liquid substance in front of him. Jova looked at it with puzzlement.   "What is it?" he asked. William smiled and said, "All the good stuff," and he took a big drink of his own glass filled with the same. Jova asked, "Is there, by any chance, any bacon and eggs in this cup?" William looked at Jova and smiled and said, "Sure, if that is what you need to believe, sure. I even threw in a jelly doughnut too. That's what is going to keep you going until lunchtime." William guzzled down the rest of his in one shot. He wiped his mouth and smiled with great satisfaction. Jova raised his glass to his lips. He caught a whiff of a berry smell and thought maybe it tastes better than it looks. As he drank down some of the con-coction and his eyes closed. He thought to himself, it is positively not a smoothie or a milkshake. The texture was very gritty. William said, "That's a fine lad, now take all these" and he placed a handful of pills in Jova's hand and handed him a large glass of water. Jova asked, "What are these pills for and what do they do?" William replied, "Does it really matter to you?" Jova looked at them and thought to himself, they can't make me feel any worse and swallowed them down.

William slapped Jova's back and said, "Let's get started. Ok, up onto the massage table you go and face down, please." He was set up near the front porch. Jova thought that maybe this won't be so bad. He ached all over, although he tried not to show it. William began to massage him. Jova felt pain and pleasure as William worked on all the sore muscles until they were loos-ened up. Towards the end, Jova felt more relaxed and less pain.

William spoke, "Let's get some stretching done." William began to manipulate Jova's body into many positions. Some of them did not look natural. Jova began to feel his body loosening up and feeling better. They began to walk around the yard.

Sally stood at the screen door peering out at them. Dude was beside her looking on too. Sally smiled and rubbed Dudes back and side. She made a pot of coffee. She stared off into nowhere as she sipped from her cup.

Janie approached the edge of the kitchen. "Is it

safe?" Janie asked in a quiet voice. Sally turned and said "They are outside. The coast is clear, and the coffee is ready." Janie drank her coffee quietly and then got a devious smile on her face. Sally began to smile at her asking, "What?" Janie asked, "Do you want to try something that is nasty?" Sally gulped, "Sorry, I'm not that way. "No!" Janie said "Not that! It is something to eat for breakfast." Sally said, "Oh, I guess so?" Janie toasted two pieces of bread. She rummaged through one of Williams bags and pulled out a small dark brown glass container. She spread the substance over some buttered toast. Janie handed Sally an exact duplicate of the toast. Janie smiled and took a bite and Sally followed. Sally's face scrunched up and then took another bite. Their faces showed no enjoyment, as they kept eating the toast. Sally stared at Janie and asked, "What is this?" Janie laughed, it's Vegemite. Isn't it, nasty tasting?" Sally got a big smile and said, "YES!" Janie smiled and asked, "Do you want another piece of toast with some more on it?" Sally thought for a moment and answered "YES, I would." Janie giggled as she made two more. They both bit into the toast and had the same odd look. Sally asked, "Why are we eating this?" Janie wiped her mouth, "I don't know why, but I have the same reaction every time I eat it." Sally smiled and asked, "How often do you eat it." Janie replied laughing, "About 3 to 4 times a week." "Where on earth did you come across that stuff?" Janie said, "It's Williams, he orders it from Australia." Sally burst out with delight and said, "OH YEAH, that song." Sally began singing, "We come from the land down under" Janie began to sing along with her. They quickly forgot the words and just hummed and then sang "he offered me a vegemite sandwich". Janie laughed. William heard that song one day, about a 6 months ago. He just upped and ordered some out of curiosity." "That's impulsive of him," Sally remarked. Janie giggled, "Yeah, he is like that."

"One night I came home, and he had silk Japanese kimonos. He was wearing one and he had one for me too. He had me in one just seconds after I walked through the door. He could barely keep from giggling, he was so tickled with himself. He had a whole sushi type of dinner laid out. Of course, it was all veggies, though. Finally, I saw something he could not do well. He could not work chopsticks for the life of him. So, I joined in with the whole thing and fed him, slowly, one piece at a time. I looked around the room and candles were everywhere. It must have taken him a half-hour to light them all."

Sally snickered, "Is he one of those guys that wants a submissive female?" Janie laughed, "Oh no, on the contrary, he doesn't seem to take to a lot of pampering from me. I think he likes to do things for others. He seems to like the response from me." Sally said, "It sounds quite wonderful, what was your reaction?" Janie had a devilish grin on her face and quite proudly she said, "We didn't make it to dessert until the morning." Sally snorted and blushed, "Oh my! I bet he does like your reactions." They both giggled together. Sally fanned her face with her hand and said, "My, oh, my. Sounds like you made the devil himself blush." Janie smiled and nodded her head and hummed mmmm-mmm, mm.

Janie stopped giggling and said, well you know they are not all home runs. He tried to do a picnic out in the country once. We drove out of the city and found a little clearing out off the main road. He placed a blanket down and the sun was shining brightly too. It was in the summer, so it was a lot on the warm side. I mean to tell you those tv shows leave a lot out. Like the minute food is out, a million bugs show up and I mean a million. I don't know what kind of flies they were, but those things were biting without mercy. You know how everyone likes a sunny day. "Well, that's nice when you're at the pool, when you can cool off with a swim. I tell you it's no fun in the middle of a field. That sun started baking us - it must have been 100 degrees that day. We both started sweating like we had run 3 miles. As tough as he is, we ended up back in the car with the air conditioning on full blast. Mother nature kicked our buts that day."

"William took a little break from the creative adventures for a little while." Sally covered her grin and said, "Poor thing, I hope he didn't give up after that." Janie abruptly answered, "OH NO, he came back really good. I should have seen it coming because he gets all mysterious and giddy, when he has got an idea brewing. One night, I got home from work and he greets me at the door with a glass of champagne. He ushers me to the bathroom to shower. When I come out of the bathroom there is this gorgeous, 18th-century looking gown, complete with shoes and accessories. I tell you what, I don't envy the work those women went through to dress like that on an everyday basis. He knocked at the door and said, 'Madame, the room is ready for your presence.' When I opened the door, he was bowing to me. I lightly slapped him on the shoulder with my hand fan. At this point, he raised his head and said 'My goddess, your beauty warms my soul. Oh, princess, may I?' Janie said, "I have to admit, he got to me. He was even dressed up in an 18th-century outfit too, with white stocking and buckled shoes. When he looked at me there was no doubt in his eyes, he meant it. He even placed a tiara on my head. He put my arm in his and walked me to the dining room, where there were silver plates with lids over them. A silver candelabra was lit and there was also a lovely bouquet of flowers. He had a bottle of champagne on ice. Strawberries, grapes, pineapple, and melon were placed on the table, too. He sat me down and held my chair for me. It was so much I almost started crying. It was so wonderful and elegant and beautiful. It was like a dream. I swear time stopped, and I wasn't sure if it was real or not. He placed one of each fruit on my plate. He grinned excessively as he watched my expression. I was so shaken. I tried to be seductive and alluring by putting the strawberry slowly in my mouth and licking it. I don't know how it looked, but I tried. After the fruit, he placed a plate in front of me. Pulled the lid off and said, 'voila - French toast, Madame.' He uncovered two enormous slices of golden bread. The smell was of banana and coconut, and it filled the room. He even a little silver sauce container, and he poured the syrup over the toast. I took a bite and it tasted astonishing. The warmth of the bread just seemed to melt away in your mouth." Janie teared up and began to cry. Sally handed her a napkin and rubbed her back.

Janie wiped her eyes and asked "Why would he do so much for me? I'm not that special to deserve such things. I'm not some kind of wealthy society princess, who probably expects things like that." Sally hugged her and said in her ear. "Sure, you are worth it, and so is he. You said so yourself, you looked into his eyes, there was no doubt, no insincerity." Janie whispered back, "It's too much, isn't it?" Sally pulled back and looked at her and said, "You found a damn good man. Although that whole no meat thing is questionable." Janie was quiet for a moment. Sally exclaimed "That's it, that's it - you were looking for something wrong with him and that's it!" Janie looked at her puzzled, and asked, "What?" Sally, with a big smile, answered, "You are looking for his flaws and the whole no meat thing is it. Granted it is not a terrible one like a cheater, or a drinker, a liar, or a gambler, etc... But you now have found it." Janie smiled in agreement and said, "Yeah, and now that I think about it, and that whole manners thing. It is a little over the top." Sally looked slightly puzzled, Janie added "I guess the manners thing is to be expected with him growing up in a military house."

Sally said, "I remember some teachers were hard on us as kids in school, but manners were mostly taught by a parent." Janie interrupted, "That's right and his father was in the military, so he must have been the strict military type. That reminds me, I was on a call once where the father was marching his kids in the rain, for like a whole day until one of the neighbors called it in, out of concern. The kids were like 8 and 10 - a boy and a little girl." Sally quietly covered her mouth with her hand while listening. Janie never paused. "The father was back from the war just 2 days. When we got there, he saluted us and said, 'The troops are ready for inspection, sir, and he stood at attention. He said they are an outstanding group, sir.' The kids never complained in his presence. When we got them alone, they were hungry, and their feet were blistered." "Oh my, what happened?" Sally asked. Janie said, "He was scooped up by military police and put in some therapy program. He got better after a little time and having someone to talk to really helped him. The children went to live with his sister for a while. Until he was able to function in civilian life." Sally asked, "Did everything work out for them?" Janie answered, "Who knows, we got no further calls from them. I hate those calls because there is no clear-cut bad guy. The father was lost in his own head and the children got dragged in there too. He did not mean to harm anyone, and other than some blisters the kids were fine."

Janie paused for a moment and asked, "Do you think something like that happened to William?" Sally looked at Janie and asked, "Has he ever talked about his childhood like it was bad?" Janie continued, "I mean, he did have the whole father being an amputee thing that we talked about last night, but I don't think there were any abusive types of things going on." Janie said, "We trailed off there for a bit, where were we? Oh yeah, 2 flaws right there. The no-meat thing and a possible freaky military father obsessed with manners. It was so obvious – Ha!" Janie began to show have a grin of satisfaction. "You are right. I know his thing now." She hugged Sally and said, "Thanks I feel better now."

Janie took off out of the house running like yesterday. Sally went to the doorway to watch her. Dude came up beside Sally and looked with great curiosity he sniffed up at the air, as they watched Janie run at full speed. William turned to face her looking amazed as she jumped and landed on him. She kissed him long and hard, again and again, and said, "I will never make you march in the rain and I am ok with the no meat thing too." She kissed him again. Jova smiled and quietly walked off saying "I think its break time."

Janie hugged William hard then pulled back and looked into his eyes. William was happily puzzled by her attention again and he whispered to her, "Were you trying to take me to the ground." She smiled and said, "I'll take you any way I can get you!" and kissed him again. He fell back on to the ground with her on top. She pulled back staring at him with her hands resting on his chest. "I love you" she said and kissed him again.

Jova walked up the steps looked at Sally and Dude, then looked back at them on the ground. He said, "I think we're done for today." Sally grinned, "I think so too." Jova drank down a glass of water. Sally came in behind him and asked, "How are you feeling?" Jova took a deep breath and answered, "Tired, but energetic at the same time." Jova drank down another glass of water. "He knows his stuff. I have noticed more of a range of motion. My legs bend more, and they have more spring in them. So, I guess you can say I am on the right path." Sally grinned, "He has got you going somewhere, even if it seems to be uphill all the way. Jova snickered and said, "You are right about that."

CHAPTER 7

WILLIAM'S DINNER AND FUDGE

That night William served dinner and stated "Don't ask what's in it. This is just spaghetti and meatballs with baked garlic bread. Everyone eat up - all I want to see is empty plates."

Sally spoke up "I can't eat this whole plate!" He looked her up and down and said, "You are due some full plates. You must have to run around in the shower just to get wet. You look like you have been running on empty for a while so, eat up. No excuses! I even brought a nice wine to help wash it down." He held up his glass to toast, "Here is to good food and wonderfully charming and beautiful women." The glasses clinked together. Sally blushed a bit and smiled.

Janie grinned and took a drink then raised her glass and toasted, "Here is to good cooks and good men with tight bottoms." Sally snorted and smiled as she clinked her glass. Sally took a small taste of the spaghetti and was pleasantly surprised, "Mmmmmmm, this is very good." Jova had plenty of appetite after his day of training. He was halfway through his plate before he stopped and looked around. He felt a little embarrassed and he slowed himself down. He wiped his mouth with a napkin and took a drink of wine.

Janie spoke up as she turned away from staring at Jova smiling, "The great thing about garlic bread is it tastes great and when your boyfriend eats it too, neither must worry about bad breath when they kiss." William smiled, "Your breath is never so bad that I won't kiss you." She looked at him and said but yours is questionable sometimes. She looked seriously at him and then slapped his upper arm. "I'm just fooling with you." He grasped his arm and made a painful face and exclaimed: "OWWWWWWWWW THAT HURTS! Stop it, you're a meanie". He sounded like a little kid on the playground. "I have a witness that saw you beating me up," he said jovially. She slapped him in the same spot. Janie asked Jova "Did you witness a slapping, detective?" Jova smiled, "Me no speaky the English." They all had a little laugh at his reply.

Sally snorted out a laugh and said, "William, may I ask what made you become a vegan?" William took in a deep breath and thought for a second. He exhaled, I guess it was all the cartoons and the wildlife shows I grew up watching. You know where the animals walked and talked like humans. I guess that was the seed. That lay dormant for a long time but then later in life as I started studying nutrition. I started reading about vegetarian diets. I started having thoughts of animals playing in a field, then someone coming over and just killing them. It seemed to get worse, like if you had to explain to the cow's children why you were going to take their mother away forever or why you were taking away someone's child. I think I kept picturing them with human thoughts and sadness. You know how you watch an animal show and an animal gives birth. The mother cleans the whole animal. She protects it, feeds it, keeps it close and warm, then teaches it how to live and survive. That seems to be the same traits of love and feelings as a human raising their kids to me. One day I just looked at the food on my plate and thought I can't take someone's baby away, not when there are so many other food options out there.

"When I see meat, I can also picture that it could be human meat. I mean what is the difference other than we have thumbs and we can talk but we are animals. I'm not really going to stop people but, I am not going to be oblivious to what's going on. The best I can do is I will not contribute to an animal's demise. I don't think my life is any worse off. Nor do I feel like I'm missing out or depriving myself of anything. I feel better for it and I think my soul is better too." Everyone's mouth hung open as they thought about what he was saying and describing. William took a sip of wine. Sally began to ask and then stopped then asked, "What about milk and cheese and stuff that you don't kill the animal for." William answered, "Well, like I said I started relating the animals to human traits. I just pictured humans in the same situation, as if you girls were forced to constantly give milk, not to mention being hooked up to machines to be milked." Sally covered her chest as he spoke and had a sour pained face.

William continued, "I mean I related it to slavery and the horrible world back then. That was so inhuman and what happened throughout history. I just put myself in that position, of just being forced with no rights to your own life and your children's lives. Your children were being taken from you and forced into servitude.

"I mean even milking a cow, there's a quaint picture of the one cow and one farmer, milking it by hand in an old barn. It's a Norman Rockwell picture if I ever saw one. The farmer carries the milk into the house for the family to consume. It is far from that picture today. There are hundreds of cows in stalls hooked up to machines. Janie and Sally covered their breasts again as they continued to listen.

"How about taking a chicken's egg? There is a baby in there. So, when they take an egg from a chicken, they literally took the chicken's unborn baby. I never understood that. Many people asked me about eating eggs, like they are not an animal at all, like it is the same as milk." William shook his head in revulsion, "Ugh. I just picture someone's little-undeveloped baby frying in the pan. Aww" His body shakes as if he were going to vomit.

Sally quickly spoke to keep him from thinking about that picture too long and for her too. As she thought about it. She asked, "How long have you been a veggie guy?" He replied, "I guess about 5 years now. You know, one of the best things now is the food." Sally asked, "In what way?" He said, "Well, there are always new ways of making old recipes now - new combinations of foods, the innovations, just experimenting in my own kitchen with different things. It becomes an adventure trying something different. I have a contest with myself to find something new that brings a face of approval from Janie." Janie snickered, "You know I always thought I wanted one of those adventurous guys, but that sometimes comes back to bite me on my ass" she said playfully. William smiled and said, "I'll admit not all of them are home runs."

"I remember my first attempts at cookies." Janie snickered again and said, "They looked like cookies until you tried to pick one up. They just disintegrated to the touch." Sally snorted a laugh and said, "I'm sorry." Janie said, "You can laugh - we sure did! we found some ingredients you just can't leave out."

William spoke, "But I came back from that with that peanut butter fudge." Janie joyfully said, "That was a good come back until, 2 weeks later, when my pants barely buttoned closed. Then fudge became a bad thing." Janie added, with sadness, "It was so good I won't let him bring powdered sugar home again, because if we have it, we could be tempted in a flash." Sally covered her mouth with her hand and asked if it is really that good? Janie smiled a devilish grin, "Oh yeah." Sally spoke up, "There is some powdered sugar here."

William sprang from his chair with great glee on his face. Janie exclaimed, "Oh no! This is the closest I have ever related to a badly hooked drug addict. Wait until you have some of this!"

William resembled a mad scientist, working in his

laboratory. He grabbed and tossed in the ingredients with no measurements checked. He just tossed it in the bowl and said, "That's close enough." William stirred a big mixing bowl and purposely kept his back to them, like playing keep away from the rest of the kids. He shaped the concoction into large squares on two round plates. Then theatrically placed them in the freezer. He cleaned up his mess and sat down.

The whole time Jova was half-asleep as he watched all the interaction with great enjoyment. He watched each one of their reactions and their emotions. He enjoyed the togetherness, like a family on a tv show. He especially enjoyed Sally's reactions, and her looks of bewilderment as she listened to William and Janie speak with such openness. It had been a long time since he had been in a normal social setting. He was comfortable with all who were there. The room felt warm, but not in temperature. It was warm in good feelings. It was so good to see Janie smiling and so relaxed. William, of course, never looks tense at all. Sally's smile was so gentle, as were her movements as she covered her mouth with the tips of her fingers, so she didn't overexpose her lovely smile, he assumed it was a habit she must have picked up from having braces. When he looked at her the room became more fragrant and brighter, like her aura spreading from her, but only his eyes saw this.

He felt good until thoughts of past experiences came to his mind. The ugly realities of the world. The horrible things that are done to people by other people.

For the most part, without a lot of malice, more like a matter of fact. People had settled on such a low standard of life. They weren't accustomed to anything better than what they had always had. It wasn't necessarily food and material objects, it was more like a lack of just common respect of life. That was the everyday life in those hard parts of the city.

Then thoughts of the bad people began to creep into his thoughts. The ones who felt they could do what they wanted to the weaker ones, as long as they didn't get caught, they didn't do anything wrong. His stomach seemed to become uneasy as he thought about the worse ones. The pure evil ones - they would do horrible things and not have a concern, regret nor any remorse, for anything they had done. His thoughts started racing towards the killer in Sally's case. The different bodies in unspeakable conditions started flashing through his mind. The blood, open wounds, faces contorted in terror.

He remembered starting down that long corridor and where he found Sally. He felt so many things at that time. He felt terrible that she was there, but he was relieved he had gotten to her before she was killed. He had empathy for what she had faced and will have to live with for the rest of her life. That whole experience will overshadow her life forever.

He remembered the killers face, it was a blur as the knife came into his thigh. His only want at that time was for Sally to get away. His leg went numb. The stabbing feeling seemed to dull away as his mind processed the overload of pain. His thoughts at the time were of her face filling with tears as he picked her up off the table. She was the only thought in his head as he tried to fight off the killer. Another stab and another and another. The killer felt him getting weaker and weaker, as the blood drained from his body. The killer began to taunt Jova, a slice on his face once then another and another. Jova trying to hold the knife hand back but not strong enough to stop him.

The killer spoke in an evil contemptable tone and said, "Another slice, and you will be like my other works. Slices here, and slices there, and you will be my only male work. Oh, how everyone will admire my work. They will just envy what I have done here today. Don't worry I will finish on that other one in time. Once I start a project, I must see it come to its completion. What kind of artist would I be for the people to see my undone works?"

Sally's face came into Jova's mind at that point and a surge of strength came over Jova. His hands had stopped the knife. The killer couldn't drive the knife into Jova, because Jova held fast like an immovable object. His arms had turned to stone. Then Jova's vision became blurry and was no longer able to focus on the killer's face.

A loud BLAM!!! and William's hand came down onto the table. "It's ready!" William said with excitement, as he got up to check on his creation. To Jova the loud sound was like a gunshot bringing his attention to the present. Jova face was wet with sweat beads. Sally and Janie looked at Jova with some concern "Are you OK?" they asked.

Jova shook it off and said, "Yeah, I'm fine, just a little tired. I think I'll turn in early." He stood up and wished everyone a good night. He wandered to the bathroom and splashed his face with cold water and stared into the mirror. He was staring into nothingness, but his face finally came in to focus, with all the scars, and he began remembering each time the killer would slice on his face, as he looked and remembered each little cut and slice. He imagined the blood starting to drip from the cuts. He stared until his image was nothing but blood. Tears of blood fell from his eyes. He closed his eyes and rubbed them with the palms of his hands. His eyes slowly opened to a face with no blood. Just scars from his past He turned on the water in the shower. He stood there with the water running over his head. It seemed to be an eternity. He dried off and found himself in his bed staring at the ceiling. He tried not to think anymore and he fell fast asleep.

Back in the kitchen, William cut up the fudge in little one-inch squares. "Sally are you ready?" She smiled and opened her mouth. He dropped a piece onto her tongue. He asked Janie, "Are you ready?" She blasted out, "Hell yes! You know it. Come on and give it to me." He dropped a piece into her mouth. Sally and Janie slowly started chewing. Their faces took on a look of great pleasure and satisfaction. "Mmmmmmmmmm" they groaned. "Oh, my goodness" Sally said with a breathy voice, "Mmmmmmmmm that is decadent, awwww." Janie smiled and breathed out a groan too, "Mmmmmmmmmmmmm" and said, "William you are going to get such a thank you tonight." Each one took one piece after another until they were all gone. All three looked like they were stuck to their chairs, so relaxed and satisfied, with eyes closed just remembering the last piece and tongues rolling around in their mouth making sure there was none left.

A moment of silence and Sally slowly began to speak, "I think I just committed a sin. My, my that was the sweetest thing I think I have ever had." They all smiled, their eyes still closed. Janie slowly spoke, "If this is what drugs are like, no wonder there are so many addicts."

William stood up slowly and laughed and said, "Drugs??? We're lucky we are not in a diabetic coma. Come on, my love take me to the end of this goodnight, so, our eyes may close together and reach the dreamland at the same blissful time." William took her by the hand and pulled her to her feet. He led her down the hallway. She just said, goodnight quietly and followed him with her eyes still closed. Sally moved to the couch. She thought to herself how tasty those sweets were. Dude walked over to her and sniffed at her. He laid down next to her on the floor.

CHAPTER 8

JUST PEOPLE

The next morning Sally was sipping coffee and Janie sauntered into the room with her well-rested smile and said good morning to all. Sally poured a cup for her. Janie took a big sip and said, "There is nothing like that first sip of coffee." Sally nodded her head in complete agreement.

William lightly knocked on Jova's door and said, "Wake up buttercup. Time to get busy. We have new things to do today." William sat down at the table, "Mmmmmmmm coffee. I have missed you since we last met," he told the cup as he held it.

Sally presented William with a bowl of oatmeal with raisin bran cereal mixed in it. William took a bite chewed it. With a great smile, he blurted out "Genius!!! What a genius combination. Outstanding Miss Sally." Sally replied, "Actually that is Jova's recipe." William said, "Well, kudos to him - I love someone who will, from time to time, take a jump from the norm and add a little friendly mischief to life."

Jova was feeling better this morning as he grabbed the cup with vigor. All of his body was sore, but not de-bilitatingly sore. The kind of good soreness your body feels after a good work out. As soon as you start moving around, the soreness falls away from your mind. Everyone seemed well-rested and in good spirits. Jova sat down slowly. Sally placed a bowl of food in front of him and smiled a good morning. Jova smiled and thanked her in a soft humble voice.

William bellowed out, "Good morning Jova are you ready for today's activities?" Jova replied, with a thumbs up and a halfhearted, "I will stand tall today and face the beast that awaits me." William said with a grin, "Very well my good man your progress is coming along very well Jova. You should be good to go in another week."

Sally patted Jova's back and continued to rub it softly. She seemed to be off in thought as she stood beside him. Her hand found itself on his shoulder as she stared out at nothing. Her grip became firmer, and firmer so tight Jova looked up at her as she continued to be lost in her thoughts, as a look of fear came over her face. Janie and William looked on with concern.

Jova loudly announced, "Sally, you did a fine job making breakfast." It startled Sally and brought her back to the present. She smiled and patted his back again and sat down at the table. Sally took a sip of her coffee and spoke with a nervous tone. She tried to cover up for her moment of insecurity, and said, "That was the recipe you showed me Jova." Jova replied "It tastes much better than how I make it." Sally focused on Jova as she replied, "Oh, I added maple syrup to it, a lot of syrup." Janie spoke up, "I can taste it in there. It is a delicious breakfast."

William took his final gulp of coffee and said, "Are you ready Jova?" Jova rose to attention and said, "I am ready to stand tall." William rose and replied, "Outstanding!" as the screen door slapped shut behind them. Janie asked, Sally how she was feeling this morning? Sally replied, "Oh just a little unfocused, I guess." Janie thought for a moment and said, "Perhaps us girls need some fresh air today - how about we go for a walk?" Sally agreed.

They walked down the driveway past the men as they contorted and stretched in all sorts of what seemed to be unnatural ways. The girl's heads tilted sideways and smiled, and each gave a little wave goodbye.

At first, they made small talk about nothing and everything. Then Janie asked, "How are you doing with what happened to you?" Sally paused for a moment and thought about evading the whole question, then she took a deep breath and said, "I want to say I am just hunky-dory but, it comes and goes. There's a grip of fear that I can't get away from. Then I think of Jova's face, his kind eyes, and it washes it all away and I begin to feel better. There is a strength I get when I see him, the courage that he has, and you too. You both go out there and face all the evil out there in the world - day after day - putting yourselves in harm's way fearlessly."

Janie spoke up, "Slow down! Don't think that! We are just people. We are afraid, and we have anxiety just like anyone else. We are trained and equipped to deal with that kind of thing. Please don't think we are fearless at all. Although we may be a bit jaded from being exposed to bad incidents, a bit more so than most people. "

Sally stopped her and replied, "I could never do what y'all do. How can little ol' me go in take down someone the size of William?' Janie burst out with a laugh and jokingly said, "Well, with him you could probably give him a sad look." Janie composed herself for a more serious thought process and said, "Look, everything has its weaknesses. You have to know where and how to exploit it. Even little you can take someone the size of William. Now I am not saying that it will be a fair fight, and you will win every time. The classic kick to the balls still works wonders - or pepper spray in the eyes. These things will usually slow down most, at least enough for you to run to safety or get away. An electric stun gun will stop them in their tracks, for sure!" Sally said, "Oh yes, I have seen those on the news. Janie gave a little giggle and said, "You better believe it. Those things are the real deal. I can show you some self-defense moves too - like using the size and weight of your opponent against them."

When they got back from their walk Janie and Sally began practicing in the yard near Jova and William. Eventually, the two groups merged into one. Days went by, and each took turns showing Sally different moves to defend herself. As Sally learned more and more, she became more confident in her own abilities. Jova became stronger and more agile with his movements.

Sally and Jova would have more physical contact as those days went on. A little hand-holding in the beginning then a hug or two and then to kisses on the cheek. Jova was at first uneasy and thought it was not a good idea to lead her on. That is what his head tried to tell him, but his heart told him something else. He began to look for those moments. Her bright smile and her soft touch gave him great comfort. Janie watched as they grew closer. At first, she just thought it was a superficial feeling Sally had for him, because of the incident. As the days went by Janie accepted there was something real there.

CHAPTER 9

STANDING TALL

As they were eating dinner one night. Sally asked, "A few days back you said something about standing tall. What does that mean?" Jova answered, in a dismissing tone, "Oh, that was an old story my grandfather used to tell me at bedtime." Sally with a surprised smile, said, "Well." A long pause captured silence from Jova. She reiterated, "Well, then share it with us." Janie and William clanked their forks against their plastic cups and said, "Yes, yes, tell us a story of your childhood memories." They all smiled at him, knowing Jova would let everyone else carry the conversations on and would listen but not contribute in sharing his thoughts. He looked at them and reluctantly answered, "Ok, ok, this is a story my grandfather was told by his father and so on."

"In a small mountain village, there lived a little boy named Sasha. He was the blacksmith's son. Sasha had a secret he kept from everyone in the village including his father. The secret was that Sasha was afraid. He was afraid all the time. The wind would blow, and tree limbs would rub together. He would freeze up and get goosebumps all over. Sometimes at night, he would hide under his bed until he fell asleep. He would have nightmares about wolves chasing him. He awoke sweating and his heart racing. Now his father loved him very much, but his father worked very hard and he had not noticed his son's problem. One day his father did not wake him for breakfast. Sasha went to his bed and found his father was very sick. His face was pale and his skin clammy. Sasha got him a cup of water and a damp cloth. He placed the cloth on his forehead. Sasha darted from the house straight to the doctor's office. He banged on the hard wooden door furiously. Finally, the door opened and there was the doctor, and he was sickly and pale too. Sasha shouted 'You must come! My father is sick, you must come now!' The doctor said, 'We are all too sick. You must go to the hermit at the base of Three Wolves' Mountain and tell him that he must give you all the herbs for the sickness. He will know what to do.' The doctor barked out to Sasha, 'Now go boy, you must be back by morning or it will be too late.' The boy began to run and run through the forest. He remembered earlier in the spring. He and his father traveled to the hermit's cave to deliver a large iron pot. His father told him 'You have nothing to fear as long as you stand tall.' Sasha thought to himself - easy for his father to say, he was bigger and stronger than most men already. Sure, it is easy for him to not be afraid. Sasha ran for what seemed to be hours. His only thought was of helping his father to get well. He started seeing things out of the corner of his eyes. Shadows moving fast and then nothing. Goosebumps flooded his skin. When he felt he could run no more he began to just walk. The forest around him became stranger with sounds of leaves rustling and branches falling from old trees. He began to tear up when the smoke from the hermit's fire caught his eye. He was finally there. There was a small shack built up against the mountain base. Sasha began to run again. He reached the weather-beaten door and began banging on it. The door flung open to a hairy, smelly old man dressed in sewn together rags.

"The boy blathered out 'Herbs need now - the doctor and my father are sick, your help now.' The hermit scratched his head and his chin under his long straggly beard. The hermit said, 'One more time boy and slow down your mouth so I may understand.' Sasha took a deep breath and blurted out, 'The doctor sent me to you - to get herbs for the fever. Everyone is sick and you know what to do and what we need.' Then Sasha collapsed. The hermit laid the boy on his own bed and he felt his head. 'Ahh,' the hermit spoke to himself, 'You are not too well either my boy. I have just the thing for you.' He grabbed a special jar on the shelf. He poured a terrible smelling ooze of liquid into a cup and poured it into the boy's mouth. Then the hermit left him to collect herbs from the forest. When he came back, hours later, the boy awoke panicked and groggy. Sasha exclaimed 'I must get back by morning the doctor said!' The hermit placed a bowl of food in front of the boy and said, 'Well you better eat this so you can be on your way.' He gobbled down every bite that was in the bowl. The hermit said, 'Not many men will travel the forest at night. The three wolves roam the forest, particularly at night. The boy looked up at the hermit and said, 'Three wolves?' The hermit said, 'The white one is named Fear. The black one is named Doubt. The silver one is named Weakness.' The boy went back and forth in his mind - the wolves and his sick father. The hermit looked at the boy and said, 'There is only one way to beat them. Did your father tell you how to?' Sasha's mind filled with all the many different things his father had told him over the years. Finally, all stopped in his mind and he heard his father's voice and it said, 'Stand tall my son, and you will have nothing to worry about, nothing to fear.' The boy blurted the words out 'Stand tall.'

"The hermit answered, 'That's right my boy. Here, you carry this bag - it has some of the cure for the sickest and some herbs. I will bring the rest as fast as my old legs will carry me.' The boy took off through the night. The moon was big and bright in the sky. There was more than enough light for Sasha to see his way. He ran hard at first, but the bag was heavy, and it slowed him down. His thoughts were on his father knowing he must get there to save him. As he made his way, the shadows began to catch his eye. The shadows began to take shapes. They were the shapes of four-legged animals. Goosebumps appeared all over him, but he continued on with purpose and determination. Then finally a shadow appeared on the path ahead of him. As he got closer, and closer the form of a wolf began to take shape. It was a silver wolf and his eyes glowed orange in the night. Sasha kept moving forward, not missing a step, until he was face to face with the wolf. Sasha stood tall and strong and faced the wolf nose to nose. Sasha told the wolf, 'Stand aside Weakness, I must pass." The wolf took a last stare into Sasha's eyes and wandered off into the forest. Sasha, although not sure just what happened, continued on with great stamina. He thought of his father who was sick in the bed. Would he get back in time? Just then, a shadowy form appeared on the path in front of him. Sasha kept moving forward, not slowing down. He saw the figure getting closer. It was a big black wolf with green glowing eyes. Sasha remembered how he had handled the silver wolf. Sasha was nose to nose with the wolf. His glowing green eyes looking deeply into Sasha's whole being. They both stood straight as an arrow. Sasha told the wolf, I don't have time for you Doubt. I have an important mission I must complete with no time for your judgment this night.' The wolf took a sniff and then wandered off into the forest. As Sasha continued on his journey, the bag growing heavier. Sasha pushed through his tired feelings. There would be time to rest later. He must get back to the village to his father and all the others relying on him, and him alone.

"The vision of everyone sick, or worse, grew clear in his mind. The forest was becoming more familiar. He was close to the village. Just then, a loud growl echoed through the forest. A growl that would stop grown men in their tracks. Heavy footsteps seem to come from everywhere. The final wolf was upon him. The sounds got closer and louder. A snarl and a growl, twigs and fallen branches breaking underfoot. The sounds were all around. Sasha stopped and he adjusted the bag. He straightened his body into a firm stance. He yelled out to the forest with strength and force and said, 'Face me Fear, I am here and I am standing tall. I will not stop, and I will not yield to you - nothing will stop me from my task.' Just then the largest white wolf leaped out and stopped nose to nose with Sasha. The wolf growled at him. Sasha looked into his glowing red eyes. Sasha growled out in a strong stern voice, 'I have no time for you Fear. I must complete my journey, and nothing can stop me but death.' The wolf gazed into Sasha's eyes and stepped to the side and darted off into the night.

"Sasha kept going and the village came into view. The moon was fading. Sasha burst through the door of his home. He quickly gave his father some of the cure. Then he went to the doctor's place and treated him. Sasha and the doctor went from house to house with the cure as fast as the doctor could make it. The hermit showed up as the roosters crowed through the village. Once Sasha had been to every home, at least one time, he came back to his own. He opened the door slowly. He stood at his father's bedside. His father's eyes cracked open slowly but sure. Sasha hugged him and said, 'Good morning father.' His father hugged him back and laughed and asked, 'Is it time for breakfast yet? I am starved.' Sasha said, 'Me too.' From that day on Sasha was never afraid again   The End."

Sally with tears running down her cheeks, gasped out, "What a beautiful story." William exclaimed, "Outstanding! A great tale of a young man coming into manhood." Janie added I must say well done Jova, well done indeed. Jova smiled as he saw everyone truly enjoyed the story. He began to reflect on the lessons of the story. Jova reached under the table to hold Sally's hand. Her face blushed as she held his hand.

William surveyed the faces in the room. "Well, it is past my bedtime, we are off to bed." He grabbed Janie by the fingertips and led her down the hallway. They giggled a bit as they closed the door to the bedroom. Janie was heard saying, "Come here, mister, and give me some sugar." They embraced and kissed and then fell onto the bed.

Meanwhile, Jova and Sally uncomfortably sat holding hands. Each knowing they wanted more. Sally turned and started to say something then stopped. Jova finally pulled her close to him and kissed her, as though they were lovers for a million years. They were both lost in the moment. She opened her eyes slowly and said, "Stand tall Jova" in a soft voice. Dude took a sniff at them and lazily walked off and laid down. Sally and Jova continued kissing their way to the bedroom. The door closed behind them. Dude put his head down for a nice long nap.

CHAPTER 10

SALLY GETS TO WORK

The next morning the sun shined on Sally's face through the window. Jova turned to her and kissed the tip of her nose ever so gently. He softly told her good morning. She kissed the tip of his nose in the same way. They gazed into each other's eyes, and Jova spoke quietly, "You said you came here to get me all better and back on my feet." She took a serious expression and nodded yes. She was quite puzzled by this. He smiled and said, "I fear I will continue to be broken, even if it is just a little bit, and he kissed her nose again. She hugged him passionately and firmly and whispered in his ear "Well, I guess I am never leaving." He hugged her back and whispered "Good.

Meanwhile, in the other bedroom, Janie stroked William's eyebrows with her finger. Slowly and ever so gently her finger followed the curves of his face. She finally asked, "Why do you do such grand gestures for me?" A silence fell over them and just a slight breath from her. She anxiously waited for his answer. His eyes remained closed as he spoke, "I am just silly like that perhaps. A bit on the retarded side." She quivered and said, "Please, no joking", as she leaned in and kissed his forehead. His eyes slowly opened to see her emotions ready to burst from her heart. "I don't know if I can explain it, it's just the way I feel it." "Please try", she pleaded, as a tear rolled down her cheek. He pulled her down and hugged her, she laid her head on his chest. He kissed her head and began to speak. "I love you." She slapped his upper arm and said, "I need more!" He took a deep breath and exhaled. "You are a strong, smart and beautiful woman. For me, it would be a treasure just to be in your presence. When I see you smile at me. When I see you truly feel what I am trying to share with you. When I see you open up and feel so much and your walls fall down and I see all of you, the inner you. I feel the glow of your soul as it radiates out of you and it touches me. I feel it so deeply. I see you feeling my love, and my being, reaching out to you."

A tear rolled down his chest from her cheek. He softly said, "Just like now," and he hugged her softly but firmly. "I feel all of you touching me. I never felt so much from another person in my whole life and I never want to feel it from anyone else. You are the one for me. I have no doubts at all, in any way. I hope that makes sense, I feel like a clumsy mule clopping down a road stumbling over rocks, when I try to express what I truly feel."

She picked her head up slightly and kissed his chest. She stared at him and kissed his lips. She softly spoke, "You were wonderful and perfect." He got a big smile on his face. He rolled her over and he kissed her forehead and then her lips - a long warm kiss that went on for a short eternity. As sweat glistened from their body's they slowly caught their breath until it was at a normal rate and their hearts slowed down to a normal pitter-pat. They lie side by side holding hands. A stillness came over them.

He burst up and began to sing "Lips like sugar, sugar kisses. Lips like sugar, sugar kisses" he leaned over and kissed her as he sang the song - her lips, her shoulder, her belly, her knee and finally her big toe. "Lips like sugar, sugar kisses", as he opened the door to the bathroom he continued singing "I wish I knew more words to that song." He smiled at her "Lips like sugar, sugar kisses" she smiled back at him. He went into the shower and sang as the water washed over him.

William opened the bathroom door and Sally was just coming out of the bedroom. William said, "Good morning Miss Sunshine, may I inquire about your hair cutting schedule today?" She replied, "good morning", and she looked at her wrist and said, "Right now is open, especially since your hair is already wet. Put some pants on and I will meet you on the front porch in about five minutes."

As Sally was cutting his hair, the putter of a scooter brought their attention to a visitor coming down the driveway. Peck pulled up on his scooter, and pulled his helmet off, his long hair falling from the confined space. With bags in hand, he walked up the steps. He stopped and bashfully asked, "You want me to put this in the kitchen?" Sally replied, "Yes, please."

As he entered, Jova's back was to him as he was pouring a coffee. He turned to face Peck and Peck froze in his mind and body. He saw Jova's face. It was a bit startling to Peck since he knew him from before the incident. The change had thrown him off his thoughts. He was trying not to be disrespectful to Jova and stare. So he tried to talk to say something to change the atmosphere in the room. Peck said in an unconvincing tone "Hey Jova, I see you got a new hair cut. It looks good. Where did you get your hair done at?" Jova did not take offense as he saw the young man was trying to work his way out of the situation, which he obviously had no experience in. Peck remembered, as he walked up the stairs, seeing Sally cutting Williams hair. Peck started to babble out stuff, trying to nervously not be so nervous. "Dop you thunk - I mean do you think your friend can cut my hair?" Jova looked away from Peck and said, "Ask her maybe she will." Peck thanked Jova, "And by the way, my parents ask about you all the time. They would love it if you would drop by some time to catch up." Jova replied, "Yeah Peck, I'll try" as he walked back to the bedroom and turned his back to Peck.

Peck peered through the screen door and felt obligated to try to get a haircut. He thought to himself, he does like his long hair now, but after talking to Jova he should inquire at least. He asked timidly, "Excuse me, Miss Sally, would it be too much of a bother to ask for a haircut? Jova said to ask you." She looked at him and smiled, "Sure thing, sweety."

She giggled a little, "I haven't had this much business in a long time." William said, "Well, you keep doing such a good job, what do you expect?" William stood up as Sally brushed the clippings away from his neck. He proudly said, "Nothing like a good hair cut to make a man feel civilized. Oh, and I love the feel of a straight razor around my ears and neck. It feels fantastic. I haven't had that treatment in years." Peck sat in the chair and Sally wrapped him with cloth up to his neck.

William asked, "Well young man what are your aspirations in this life?" Peck spoke slowly at first, but confidence grew as he talked. "Well sir, after growing up in the grocery business, I would like to go to college and learn more about business and perhaps take some management classes. Oh, and I would like to take some English classes - I would like a better handle on words, and the proper way to communicate using them. That way I could help my parents at our store. I may be able to expand, it and add some services to it, to make it more successful. I hope to take over for them so they can retire and go traveling." Sally spoke up, "That sounds nice, do they talk about traveling a lot?" "No," Peck replied, "But they have been at the store every day for as long as I have lived. Besides that, I hear the way they talk about the different places in the movies they watch - like Rome and Paris and other exotic locations. I get the feeling like they would like to go there. So, If I was responsible enough to run the store, where they wouldn't worry about it, they could maybe go to Paris, and eat at one of those outside café places or something like that."

William wiped his eyes and sniffled a little and in a broken voice said, "That's beautiful Peck. Just beautiful." William walked away wiping his face. Peck looked puzzled, and asked quietly "Is he okay?" Janie spoke up, "Yes, he is fine, he is just a little bit on the sentimental side." Sally snorted out a laugh and covered her smile, and said with a grin, "A little?" Janie smiled, "Well okay a lot." Peck said "I think that's the first time I have ever seen a grown man cry, especially that big of a man. Well, I guess when you're that big you can do whatever you want to."

It got quiet and Sally was well into the haircut when Peck burst out saying, "Oh yeah, I like my hair on the long side, so please don't cut it too short. I really appreciate this since the town barber passed away a month ago. My dad owns the building the barbershop is in, but he doesn't know anything about cutting hair. He had bought it to help out old Tilt Johnson the town barber. Hey, you know, you should talk to my dad about opening the shop up and running it. Wait, wait, oh, oh, oh", Peck was bursting with excitement, "Would you let me present you like my idea. I could show my father how I am responsible, and I am business savvy. This will be my first business venture. This is so cool! This is what they mean by seeing an opportunity and jumping on it."

Janie grinned from the boy's excitement and the fact that most of Peck's hair was gone. He didn't notice it at all. He was deep in his mind all about the barbershop and Sally being the best barber in town. Beside the point, it was the only barbershop in town. Sally pulled the towel from Peck's chest and brushed off his neck and collar. Peck jumped from the chair and said, "The big guy was right - I do feel better and civilized. Miss Sally, will you please come now and see my father? It will be the perfect presentation with a fine new hair cut too. I can't miss with this. It will be epic. Please, please." Sally pinched his cheek and said, "Yes, yes but you have to know I am not that experienced." Peck cut her off with "Don't worry, I will handle it all. You just let me do the talking." Peck was on his scooter before Sally could say anything. "I will see y'all in like ten minutes at the store!" He drove away without waiting for a reply. Janie excitedly said, "Well I am driving. We need more coffee and some other not meat related stuff and I really want to see this play out." Sally grinned, "What do I do? I only know how to do one hair cut - the big boy hair-cut." Janie said with glee, "I noticed that too, but don't worry, he is going to handle it." Sally snorted a small short laugh out loud and said, "I don't want to make the boy look bad in front of his father."

Janie and Sally entered the grocery store. Peck burst out of the office with his father in hand and Peck exclaimed, "Here she is, I found the best barber, and plus she is really pretty too!" Sally blushed and hid her smile with her hand, while Peck talked her up. The father looked at Peck's hair cut and back at Sally several times. Then he pointed his finger up at the sky. Peck stopped talking.

The father looked like he was thinking of the greatest and most important idea in the world. Out of the silence, the father spoke, "Say, you're Jova's friend, aren't you?" Sally answered respectfully, "Yes sir," The father thought for another moment. "Ok, follow me for a spell while I consider this." Peck began to lead the way out. The father said, with authority, "Peck you are in charge here until I get back, or your mother tells you to do something." "YES SIR, YES SIR," he replied, with great importance in his voice and stance. Janie said, "I am gonna do some shopping, I'll wait here for you." Sally turned to her puzzled about what she had gotten herself into and answered, "Ok." They walked across the street to a small strip of old storefronts, with the old - fashioned barber pole spinning light mounted on the end unit. An old diner/coffee shop was in the center and a tailor/cleaner on the other end. They walked in silence. The father stopped at the door and unlocked it with a key from his pocket. He sat down in the first barber's chair and said "Ok, cut my hair."

Sally said nothing she just looked around to take an inventory of what was there to work with. She shook a cape out with a pop and pulled it snug around his neck. He began to talk, "How is Jova? doing I haven't seen him in months. You know, I never introduced myself, at least I don't think I did. My name is Samuel Taylor and you met my wife, the lovely Rose, the other day when you were in the store. "Sally answered, "Yes, I did, and my name is Sally Ann." He cut her sentence off, "Well Sally, do you use straight razors? Like in those old westerns? Do you do shaves with shaving cream and a brush too? Will you trim a man's ear hair and eyebrows without him feeling embarrassed about it?"

She cut away at Samuels' hair and listened to him ask her questions. In a roundabout way, he was telling her that was how she was going to be doing things. She answered yes to all. "You know me and Jova's grandfather was good friends. We sat in here many a Monday morning reading the papers, talking about how the weekend ball games and so forth went. We talked about Jova, and we both worried that city life was too fast for him to make a happy life. You know I had offered Jova the job of police chief here." Sally spoke up, "No, I did not know that." Sam touted himself, "Yes, I am on the town council and I had already felt everyone out on him being the chief. So, it is a done deal, providing someone else don't come along. Sally said, "You know, I like the thought of him patrolling around here and keeping everyone safe."

Meanwhile, Janie slowly walked down each aisle of the store. She looked everything over carefully. Every so often, Peck would pop up on her and ask, "How do you think it's going? I am sure it's going well," never giving Janie a chance to answer. Finally, Janie stopped him on his third time coming up to her and said with a stern voice, "Focus on what you are supposed to be doing." He composed himself. "Yes mam." He grew silent, then he excitedly said, "Miss, we have some lovely cuts of beef and it is fresh too. Maybe some fresh sausage, or pork chops - they are really good." Janie smiled and said, "No thanks, I am a vegetarian." Peck responded with, "Oh, well we have fish and seafood too." Janie smiled and said, "Sweetie, vegetarians don't eat any kind of animals. Well, I guess some run around saying they are vegetarians but eat seafood, but neither here nor there, William and I do not eat anything that was or is going to be an animal." Confusedly Peck asked, "Well what do you eat then?" Janie, in a tired response to a question she has answered too many times before, replied, "All the other food that is left - you know vegetables, fruits, beans, bread, pasta, nuts." She always thought it was on the stupid side based on her knowing there was so much out there to choose from, but she thought the same things, and asked the same questions, before she became vegetarian too.

Just then Samuel came into the store. "Well, what did you decide?" Peck asked with great anticipation. As Samuel approached, Janie noticed right off his hair was cut just like Pecks, which brought a grin to her face. Sam said, "Well son, you were right, she is a good barber and she is a good fit, too. She tried to strong-arm me a little, with some business negotiations, but I think we all worked out a good deal. She will do it for a month and at the end, we will sit down again." Peck questioned his father saying, "A month?" "Yep," answered the father, "Either the town will hate her or love her. Based on her and this fine haircut, I think everyone will love her. Besides that, there is already a line of all the guys who were at the diner. As they saw me talking to her, they walked in and complimented my haircut and started shouting they were next - like kids claiming a ride on a roller coaster. Even old Sideways Ollie had a smile on his face, and I haven't seen him smile since he could stand up straight." Peck clarified to Janie he has some kind of spine disorder. Janie nodded her head in understanding as she looked on with astonishment. Rose came in from the back and asked what all the fuss was about?

Samuel stood straight and faced her and spoke strictly, "Our son has something he would like to tell you." Peck stood up straight, just like Samuel, and at that moment anyone could see they were father and son. Peck cleared his throat and said, "Well, Mom, the town has the best new barber." Just then the father leaned over and hugged him. "Our boy has done a great job in putting this whole deal together all by himself. Rose hugged him and said, "That is a fine thing!" as she happily fussed over his new haircut. "Well, I should have known. Just look at the both of you with those handsome haircuts."

The two men went back into the stock room together, patting each other on the back, telling each other how great everything was. Rose watched with adoring eyes as they walked away. Then she turned to Janie and said, "Did you see that? This is a good day. I am so glad the boy finally got a haircut. He had such long hair, he looks more professional now. You know I was worried he was gonna join a rock band or something with that look he had going on.

I am sorry for me going on about my son like that. Is there anything I can help you with Miss?" Janie smiled, "I think I am all ready to checkout now." Rose replied in a friendly voice, "Sure thing young lady. I don't believe I have met you before are you new in town?" Janie replied, "Oh I am staying over at Jova Zarn's place."

Rose got a happy look on her face, "Oh that boy he is a fine one. How is he doing? I heard he got hurt a little bit. Peck told me he was up and around and kept saying he was fine." Janie answered, "Well he certainly took one for the team, but my boyfriend is here too, helping him recuperate with some physical therapy and rehabilitation techniques he knows. He is doing much better now." "That is just wonderful news" Rose said. "You tell him I expect to see him soon and he is in our prayers. I sure wish he would take the police chief job here. We have been hoping he would change his mind." Janie answered, "Well we sure will talk to him about everything you just said." Rose said, "You have a nice day miss", as Janie exited the store.

As Janie placed the bags in the trunk she looked down and across the street for the barbershop. She drove up to the front of the diner and parked. The barber pole was slowly turning as if it would stop at any minute from old age. Janie opened the door where she found a bunch of old men sitting and jabbering on about anything that would spark a conversation. A fellow was just getting out of the barber's chair and thanking Sally profusely for the haircut. He was leaning over as he shuffled out the door. He smiled at Janie as he passed. "You must be Sideways Ollie Janie said. The man replied "Well, yes, yes, I am but how did you know that?" Janie said, "The word is out that you have the best-looking haircut in town. He turned back to the fellows in the shop and said, "You hear that boys?" The hot girls are talking about me again!" He laughed with satisfaction as he shuffled down the sidewalk.

Janie surveyed the room. There was a big pile of hair around Sally's feet. Sally looked happy, over-whelmed and confused, all at the same time. Janie grabbed a broom from the corner and cleared away the hair. Janie said, "Well, town barber what time do you get off?" Before Sally could answer, an odd fellow came over with a dustpan in his hand and in a soft bashful voice said, "The sign says 5 o'clock, 5 o'clock the sign says, and I am next, next I am." He bent over holding the dustpan in front of the pile of hair. "Ok, sweep it on in here, on in here sweep. I am ready, ready I am", he told Janie as though she was a child. Janie was going to make a smart remark until she realized the fellow was slow, or something was going on with him. She swept some of the hair into the pan. He then slowly stood up-right and carefully maneuvered the pan of hair as if it was a stack of priceless glasses on a tray and dumped it into the trash can. Then he came back and bent over and repeated, "Ok sweep it on in there." The other men watched and some continued to read the paper. Janie swept the rest into the pan. Again, the fellow moved as though there was a stack of plates to the ceiling. One man said, "Good work Martin." The others all com-mented "Yep good job Martin. You got it all done." Mar-tin stood proud and sat in the barber's chair. "You do it well - like Ollie's haircut, please thank you." He sat in the chair smiling, nodding his head yes. "Good like

Ollie's haircut" he repeated. Sally dipped her comb in a container of blue fluid and began combing his hair. Sally turned to Janie, "I guess you could pick me up at five." Martin interrupted "Yes, yes, the sign says 5 o'clock, 5 o'clock the sign says. Been that way for a long time until Tilt went away - yep Tilt went away did you know Tilt? He was a barber like you but not exactly like you. He was a man and you are a lady. So, you are different from Tilt. Tilt went away. Did you know Tilt?" Sally answered, "Nope, I never met Tilt, he sounds like a good guy though." Martin quickly replied, "Oh yes, Tilt was a good fellow, oh yes, he was a good fellow. One time he took me bowling and we bowled. We bowled, and we even played the pinball machine. That's how he got his name Tilt, from playing a pinball machine. He told me one time he was playing the pinball machine and he pushed it too hard and it stopped playing. Then everyone called him Tilt." Sally gently said, "Well, God bless Tilt wherever he is." The group of men all said amen to Tilt. Janie felt strange in the surroundings as she watched everything and everyone. Janie broke from her amazement to say, "Ok I will pick you up at five" then Martin began talking again about 5 o'clock.

Janie whispered to her, "Here is my cell number - call if you need me and I will come." As Janie was leaving, Martin told Janie she did a good job sweeping the hair. A fine job some of the other men joined in saying, a fine job. As Janie drove back to Jova's, she thought to herself, wow, so this is what the normal people are like. At first, she thought the place was really weird, the way people talked so openly. Never in the big city would people talk to a stranger so much. Then it dawned on her, the common factor everyone was nice to her and to each other. In the big city, the slow guy Martin, would have been berated to the point he never spoke in public again.

She pulled up to the house and the guys were on the porch drinking ice water. They both grabbed a bag from her. "Where is Sally?" Jova asked. Janie laughed a little and said, "She is the town barber as of an hour or so ago, and she gets off at five o'clock. Martin made sure of that." Jova cracked a smile and giggled "Oh you met Martin." Janie replied "Yes, I did, and he helped me with my pile of hair. We did a fine job too, as the crowd can testify to. Jova laughed, "Yes Martin will help you until the job has been completed."

"Also, Peck is the up and coming businessman of the town. His parents were tickled pink about their boy getting a haircut. Of course, they would love to see you. Oh, and a side note Rose wanted to know your answer on being police chief?" Janie was mocking, angry, excited, "That's huge Jova, why didn't you tell me you got an offer like that.?" Jova replied "I wanted to finish that case first. You know how I was then." Janie said sarcastically, "Yes like a junkie looking for a fix and sometimes you smelled like one too." Jova laughed, "I am back on a regular daily cleansing basis now."

Jova grew quiet for a moment. He looked at William and Janie and he stood up straight and asked them, "Do you think the public will respect me and take me seriously with the way I look now?" "Sure! they would!"

Janie said without a pause. "You don't look that bad. I am telling you the truth." William concurred and said, "Look, if you are good at your job which you are one of the best, people will take you seriously and respect you no matter if you got a couple of scars or not." William asked sincerely, "Would you be disrespectful to a cop or a service person with one arm or one leg?" Jova replied, "Hell no!" Then, William asked, "Do you think you are the only person who would answer that question that way?" "No!" Jova answered. "Well there you go," William said with great confidence. "Once people get used to you, and the way you are, all that superficial crap will go away." "I saw many parents and loved ones deal with that stuff. I am not going to lie to you. Some do react to it poorly. Most times it's the person coming to terms with their own mortality. They see themselves in your place and think they couldn't survive what you went through. They don't think they would be strong enough to handle it. And like most people, they will turn what you are going through and make it all about them - how they are dealing with your new appearance or your new handicap. It's kinda funny strange, how people turn everything into how it is affecting them. You become a small part of the whole situation. They go from someone has hurt their baby, to get the house in proper order. They can go from those points real fast sometimes." I hear the kids apologizing for getting hurt because they don't want to put their moms to any extra work on their account. Somewhere in all of that, they find they are thankful that the person is still in their lives and they love them. Well, I have rambled on, as

I do on occasion, especially when I talk about people and their mannerisms and behavior. I digress, Jova, you just do a good job and if someone gives you grief, write them a badass parking ticket." They all began to laugh at that point. Jova raised his glass "Cheers - here's too badass parking tickets!" and they began laughing again.

That night at dinner, Sally rejoiced in all the people she met today. She told everyone at the table of Sideways Ollie, Two Times Martin, Professor Ronson and how he worked hard to become a professor at university. "I now know whose feet have corns. Oh, and the most important thing, who is single in the town - at least the men who are. That was made clear to me several times each cut." William raised his glass "Here's to the new hot barber in town." Sally blushed and smiled.

They all toasted and clanked their plastic cups and said cheers. Sally was for once the bashful one getting all the attention. Sally then perked up to change the subject. "Police chief, I like the sound of that!" Sally said. Janie smiled at Jova conveying her thoughts of encouragement to him with just a look.

CHAPTER 11

JANIE'S UNCLE BEBOP

At dinner that night William asked, "Ok, after last night's wonderful tale from Jova, who has some sort of tale or memory they would like to share with the group tonight?" The table grew silent.

Janie apprehensively began to speak. "When I was a young girl, around eight years old, my mother passed away. The two of us were the only girls in the immediate family, and we had a special bond because of that. Mom would love to piss my brothers off and say it's a girl's thing when they would barge in on us. We had our own special club and we did secret girl things. We would go window shopping and she would point out dresses and fashions. She would show me all sorts of so-called girly things. We would go and get our hair cut on a Saturday morning. Then we would go to the fancy tea house and have tea and cake. She made me feel like the most special girl in the whole world. Then one day she was taken from me. Some dumb ass bank robber was trying to get away from the police, and a stray bullet caught her in the back from two blocks away. She lay beside her car with the keys in her hand and bled out. Janie paused and took a breath to compose herself, and William reached to hold her hand under the table.

She continued, "On the night of the wake, I was so scared and felt so lost. She was not there to guide me through this, to show me what to do. So many adults were everywhere talking to my father and brothers. Strangers were everywhere. Some looked familiar - they may have been over to our house before then. I found myself sitting way in the back by myself. I never felt so alone.

"Finally, as I was looking down at the floor, out of a sea of people these super shiny black shoes appeared. I looked up and it was a police lady. She was wearing brilliant white gloves. Beside her was my Uncle Bebop. He knelt down, so our faces were the same height, and he leaned in and kissed my forehead. 'How are you doing Janie Cakes?' As he talked, I kept staring at the police lady. She was straight and perfect.

"Uncle Bebop told me 'This is my dear friend Olivia.' She knelt down and smiled at me. She reached out her bright white-gloved hand to shake mine. After we shook hands, she smiled at me and said, 'It is wonderful to meet you, young lady.' Uncle Bebop in a quiet voice asked, 'Janie Cakes would you help me if I asked you to do something for me?' I nodded my head yes. Again, he asked quietly, 'It is a big something.' I nodded yes again. 'Ok, this is it!' he said with great mystery, 'Please don't tell anyone this, but I am scared to walk up to the front and see your mom. Would you hold my hand, so I won't be so scared?' I looked at him and over to Olivia, and she nodded yes, to reassure me too.

"I stood up from the chair and Uncle Bebop rose

from his kneeling position and was towering over me. His giant hand wrapped around my tiny little hand. He would stop every so often and ask me, 'Are you sure it is ok?' I would answer him with a strong nod yes. He would thank me for helping him to not be scared. Finally, we were there, standing hand in hand at the casket. His hand grew firm like a stone. He turned to me and picked me up in his arms, our faces side by side. He kissed my cheek and said, 'Thank you for helping me come up here.' I hugged his thick neck.

"His hand reached out and touched my mother's hands and he spoke softly. 'My sweet sister, you have gone away to heaven where you can keep a better eye on all of us. We will always remember you are watching over us. We will remember all the many things you shared and taught us. We will try to be strong like you, and be the best people we can be. We will, every once in a while, go get our hair done on a Saturday and have tea and cake.' I was surprised that he knew about our special girl day thing. I thought no one knew and it was a girl's super-secret. He ended with, 'We are better people because of you being in our lives.' He turned to me and asked me, 'Well, do you think we should say anything else to her?' I whispered in his ear, and he spoke the words, 'We miss you, Mommy come back soon, we love you.'

"As we turned and walked back, I asked him how did he know about the secret Saturday girl stuff? He answered, 'That is why this police lady is here. She told me in confidence, so I could ask you something very important. You see, she too doesn't have a great girly friend and wanted to know if you would like to join her for a secret girly Saturday thing this Saturday.' The police lady smiled at me and said, 'Please?' Uncle Bebop leaned away from the police lady so only I could hear him and said, 'You see, I need you to do me this favor I really like the police lady and maybe while you two were out doing your super-secret thing, you could tell her I am a good uncle and how I was good to hang out with and do stuff with. Oh yeah, and whatever you say, don't tell her about that day we ate beans and I made those loud noises in my pants!' Just then I burst out laughing and said loudly, 'You farted, Uncle Bebop, that was so funny.' Oliva tried to cover her mouth that was grinning ear to ear. I said, 'Ok, I will, I can do that for you.' He had a big smile of relief on his face. 'Now, remember you tell her Uncle Bebop is a good guy that doesn't fart.' I laughed again and said, 'Ok that is what I will say.'

"From that point on Olivia and I would get together once a month for special secret girl day. She is the reason I became a cop and I was the reason she and Uncle Bebop got married too.   The End"

As Janie looked around for approval for the story she told, Sally grabbed a handful of tissues and handed William one too. They all began to clap their hands as if they were at a play. Sally burst out with, "That was such a beautiful story. William added, "Yes, yes, so beautiful!" as he pulled Janie near him and kissed her cheek. "I would like to meet this Uncle Bebop, too. He sounds like quite the man's man." Jova asked, "Do you know how he got the nickname Bebop? I like that nickname." Janie replied with a smile, "Well, he was always a big fan of 50's music. Apparently, when he was young, he used to always sing this song, that went like this, 'Bebop a Lula she's my baby, bebop a Lula, I don't mean maybe.' Jova said, "Yeah, yeah, I remember hearing that once or twice on the oldies station."

Sally's hand found Jova's hand under the table as they talked about the story. Janie had never shared so much of herself with a group before. While she felt sad about her mom passing, she reveled in the fond memories of her family being strong and sticking together afterward. Janie added, that her brothers, while still rough and tumble boys, always looked out for her and her father. "While you could see a sadness in his eyes for the rest of his days. He would still put on a brave face every day and reassure his family everything was just fine and dandy. He would always straighten our collars when we left for school in the morning. Like a final inspection, we would line up and he would brush off the boy's shoulders and kiss me on the head and send us on our way."

CHAPTER 12

JOVA TAKES THE JOB

The next morning, everyone awoke and greeted each other over morning coffee. Sally grabbed things in a rush and that old familiar feeling hit her and she liked it. She was going to work, just like a normal day in her life. She exclaimed, "Oh my goodness! I am going to be late." William laughed, "That is the one thing the boss does not have to worry about. "Sally stopped and smiled. "That's right - I am my own boss now." An air of pride filled her stride as she kissed Jova goodbye and Janie followed her out. "I will give her a hand getting set up", and she kissed William goodbye.

As they drove off William loudly clapped his hands together and began rubbing them together. "Well, it is just the boys today." Jova's smile showed he was unsure what exactly that meant. William burst out, "How about a light easy run from here to the grocery store and back?" Jova pulled a hooded sweatshirt on and sweatpants and tied his running shoes. He took a deep breath and announced he was ready. William smiled and said, "Excellent."

The distance to the store was only three or four miles. Jova used to walk it all the time as a kid. On occasion, he would walk it to think out a problem or a case. William was quiet for the first mile then he asked, "Are you really considering the police chief job?" Jova had thought about many things including that option. "Yes, I have", he said in a winded voice. As they got closer to town, Jova pulled the hood up over his head. William noticed it, but chose not to address it. William spoke again, "It sounds like a slower-paced lifestyle - a man could probably have enough time to start a family, even enjoy the company of others in his life. Jova looked at William perplexed, "What are you getting at?" William stopped Jova and they stood on the shoulder of the road. William looked at Jova and said, "Well, this is going to sound a little wrong or manipulative. I was thinking, if you took the job, you could bring Janie in as your second. Then I wouldn't worry about her so much. I know it is terrible for me to think about interfering with her career like this. I don't know what I would do if something were to happen to her. We are ready to start a family too." Jova spoke up, "You know a cop can get hurt anywhere - it is part of the job." William cut him off and said, "I know that, but at least here, I could have a false sense of security. Besides that, I now know you would have her back and that means a lot to me. On top of all that, you know, it is twenty times the population back in that city and that means twenty times more the chance something bad could happen." Jova looked at William's face and he saw a true concern there.

Jova thought silently for a moment. William smiled and said, "You know, Sally would have a good life here too. Shoot, Sally has already got a job here and will be rooted in this town just like you are. It is plain as the day is long, you two are in love with each other. I'm just not sure if you two know it yet." William continued, "Sally is just about the perfect woman, except for that meat-eating thing that she has going on." Jova laughed, "Yes that is an imperfection." William laughed too, "Maybe with some time I could fix that for you, ha, ha?" William nodded his head yes. Jova replied, "She is just perfect the way she is, you stick to your woman and I will stick to mine." William burst out with, "So you can say it out loud - she is your woman and she is perfect the way she is MMMMMMMMM. Let us think about what you just said out loud as a matter of fact." William smiled as if he uncovered the great secret of the ages. Jova said, "Ok, ok, you got me! When we get to the grocery store, I will talk to Samuel." William grabbed Jova and hugged him clear off the ground, "Thanks, thank you!" Jova happily said, "Ok, ok calm down, you overly excited bear cub. Let's finish this run out before you start building white picket fences everywhere."

They continued on the run. William smiled the whole way while Jova had thoughts of a happy life with Sally. When they came to the edge of the parking lot, Jova noticed a car sitting in front of the entrance to the store. Jova stopped William in his tracks. Jova spoke very clearly and sternly, as he pointed down toward the barbershop and said, "Now I need you to run to the barbershop and tell Janie there is a possible robbery in progress here. Tell her and she will know what to do!" William said, "I can help you." Jova said with great seriousness, "NO! go and go now!" William ran off to get

Janie.

Jova pulled the hood over his face. He moved up on the car in the blind spot, so the driver couldn't see him until it was too late. The driver saw a figure in his mirror, and he told Jova "Get out of here, homeless, before I put a hurting on your sorry ass. The brazen tough guy began to open his door as if to continue to ward off Jova. The driver was almost fully out of the car door, when Jova moved in fast and pulled the driver face-first into the side of the car. He tried to regain his footing, but he was dazed from the hit. Jova then wrapped his arms around the driver's neck and held him tight until he was unconscious.

He laid him down to the ground and took the keys out of the car. He then made his way to the back of the store, where luckily the trash door was open. Jova moved through the stock room quietly and with great care. Jova found Rose hiding behind some boxes. She saw Jova and began to move towards him, but he motioned to her to stay still and quiet. He moved to get a look through a crack in the doors that led to the store. There were two men, and both had guns. One had a sawed-off double-barrel shotgun with a pistol grip. The other had a pistol. Samuel and Peck were face down near the register. One man was trying to open the cash register. He was pushing all the buttons in frustration. The other was moving back and forth through the store looking down the aisles, sometimes almost to the door, Jova was at.

Jova told Rose in a quiet voice, as he led her to the

back door, "I need you to call out for me as though I was Peck, and say you need some help back here." Rose was scared and when she tried to talk nothing came out. She quietly cleared her throat and said, "Jova! You come on back here and give me a hand with these boxes." The gunman became overly alert and asked Samuel who was back there. Samuel replied, "It is just my wife. She is alone back there and needs some help from me or my son to move something. She is no trouble she is no threat to you." The gunman motioned to his partner to check it out. He aggressively flung the door open to the storeroom. It was considerably less light compared to the rest of the store. The gunman's eyes took time to adjust to the darkened space. Before he could fully make out anything clearly, Jova's hand grasped his gun hand and twisted it hard and fast and down went the gunman. The gun fell to the floor. The gunman had to follow Jova or risk his arm breaking. Jova came back towards the gunman and wrapped his arms around his neck and squeezed until finally the gunman was out like a light. Jova took the gunman's coat and put it on. The coat had a hood and he pulled it up over his head as he picked up the gun. He checked the magazine for bullets - it was loaded and ready. He backed out of the door dragging the unconscious gunman.

The final gunman looked over and saw him dragging someone out. "Did you get someone, Chomper? Chomper is the toughest, he took another one out. Leave that loser on the floor he is out. We own this store, Chomper, ain't that right." The final gunman was overconfident with his declaration of being in charge of the situation.

Jova had to move close enough to get a good shot if he had too. The gunman said, as if he was addressing an audience, "Chomper, tell them losers we own this joint." Just then Jova spun around facing the final gunman. Jova brought the gun up and aimed it at the gunman's chest and yelled with authority. "DROP THE GUN!" The gunman was stunned it was not his partner Chomper facing him. As he realized that, it sunk in. He had some panic to his thoughts. He stared at Jova and even more fear set in. He said, "Holy crap! Scarface is in the house!" trying to cover up the fact he knew he had a big problem. Jova told him again to "PUT THE GUN DOWN NOW"! The final gunman tried to talk his way out of it, "Come on Quasimodo, these people don't care about you. Why are you taking a chance for them? Join up with me and I can hook you up with some bitches? I mean I am sure you do just fine on your own and stuff. Maybe me and you working together, we could up your quality." The gunman was trying to figure out his next move. The people were all down on the floor. There was no cover for him to hide behind. He looked in Jova's face and he knows he is not going to win, and he is not talking his way out of it.

Janie is outside the front entrance with a gun. She watches Jova for a signal. Jova is frozen like a stone statue, waiting for the wrong movement. For what seemed to be a long time, the gunman goes quiet and stares at Jova. Then the gunman slowly points the shotgun at himself, breaks it open to let the two shells fall onto the floor and raises his hands over his head. Janie comes in and moves in to take the gun from the gunman. Then more police enter and handcuff the man and take him away. Jova finally loosens his stance and takes off the coat and says with relief, "Gees, that thing is hot and smells like it was dipped in cologne and ass." The gunman looked back at Jova as he was being led away and said, "Yo, yo, yo, Quasimodo, I have to give you the props. You are a fearless beast."

Rose burst out from the stock room. She screamed, "Are my men ok? Peck? Samuel?" They came up from the floor. "We are fine Princess Ann," Samuel said, with quite the relieved voice, and added "I think someone in this area I am standing in is probably going to need some new underpants. Now I am not naming names nor pointing a finger." Samuel's thumbs were pointing at himself while he finished his statement. Rose exploded in happy tears of joy and said, "I'll buy you a whole twelve pack of new ones, in any color you want!" Rose, Samuel, and Peck all hugged each other. They were so happy they were all in one piece. Janie came over to Jova and said, "Good work officer I don't think I ever saw someone stand so tall as you just did." Jova smiled and replied, "just like the academy taught us, huh?"

Outside the front entrance, you could hear policeman yelling, "SIR YOU CAN'T ENTER PLEASE GET BACK! "We are going to need some back up here this giant guy is trying to enter the crime scene." Janie told Jova with a grin, "Ok I got to go take care of this." "SIR PLEASE STAY BACK" you could hear as Janie opened the front door. Then you could hear Janie's voice, loud through the door, "WHO IS OUT HERE CAUSING A PROBLEM? SIR, DON'T MAKE ME HAVE TO HURT YOU, SIR!" Then you could hear Williams voice "Yes officer, I am sorry, please don't hurt me again."

Rose turned and hugged Jova and kissed him on the cheek and said, "Thank you, you beautiful man" and she kissed him on his other cheek "God bless you." She leaned back and brushed her hand on his cheek. She said, "You need a shave." Then she yelled out, "PECK! Get Jova the best razor and shaving cream we have and bag it up for my friend Jova, no charge!" She smiled and kissed him again, and hugged him. Samuel spoke up, "Hey, hey watch it with my best girl." Jova smiled, "You know she's all yours that's why you get the new underpants and I get the razor." They all laughed. Just then Sideways Ollie came shuffling out from the bathroom door looked around and asked, "What did I miss?" He peered around at everyone and said, "Hey Jova, I haven't seen you in a month of Sundays. Oh yeah - big news Jova there is the prettiest new barber gal in town, and she does a bang-up job. Look at how good my haircut is!" he said so proudly. He almost stood straight when he told the story. He patted Jova's back as he passed and said, "Come by the diner sometime and I will buy you a cup of coffee. Alright, I am off", and he shuffled off and out of the store.

The door opened again, and Sally stepped in she calmly walked over to Jova and smiled and hugged him and said, "Can't let you out of the yard, can we?" He hugged her back and kissed her and said in a soft voice, "I missed you. How have you been?" She smiled at him. He grabbed her softly by the hand and led her away from everyone. "I want to ask you something." She looked very serious at him "OK go ahead" she said. "What do you think about me being the police chief here in town?" She looked puzzled at him, "Why are you asking me?" He cleared his throat and looked around and then back to her. "Well, you are my girl, so shouldn't you have some input about my job change?" She snorted and giggled "I know I just wanted to hear you say, my girl." She playfully slapped his chest. He smiled and said, "Come on, what do you think?" She looked at him and said, "Any decision you make, I will accept gladly and, on that note, anything that makes you safer and around me more, I like better." He kissed her again. "Okay, I must talk to Janie for a bit, but I will see you back at the house after work, ok?" Sally said, "Work! Oh shoot, I better get back to the shop or Martin will sweep the color right off the floor.

Jova motioned to Janie to come over where no one was around. He asked her, "Janie I need you to do something for me and it's a Biggy. I want you to be my second here. I want to take the police chief job. Would you?" She looked a little stunned at him, "Wow that is a big one!" He looked at her "I really need you on board with this." Janie said, "Well, I will have to run it by William to see if this is ok with him too, as a courtesy." She straightened herself up. "You know I am going to make my own decision, but he should at least feel like he had some input too. You know I wouldn't want to hurt his fragile male ego." Jova nodded "Yes, sure that sounds good" he said slowly and unsure. Jova approached Samuel and said, "Ok I will meet you at the Diner at 5 o'clock for my decision on the job." Samuel smiled and answered "I will wear my new underpants then, and here take the razor and shaving cream. Rose will get mad if I didn't make sure you took it as a gift. Besides that, Peck had to walk all the way over there to the male grooming aisle and bag it up for you.

That evening, Jova entered the Diner at five o'clock. Janie stood beside him. They were both in their dress blues. Their shoes shined so much, if the sun were to hit them just right, they could blind a person. They stood tall and straight, side by side. The diner was filled with town leaders and elders. Samuel was at the center of the mass of people. He stepped forward and said in a clear loud voice. "The town council has convened - will the council come to order."

The room grew quiet as Samuel spoke again, "As town spokesman, I officially ask Jova Zarn to become our police chief and protect us and not give out too many parking tickets to the town council members, unless they start acting like asses." Sideways Ollie broke the silence with a "Hey Jova, I'll buy you that coffee now." Samuel cleared his throat loudly and stared at Ollie. The room grew silent again. Jova spoke, "I will accept the job on two conditions. One, Officer Janie Mazerick is my second. Samuel spoke, "You mean the officer that helped you in your apprehension and subduing of those three scoundrels? The officer that helped you save several prominent and handsome key townsfolk?" Ollie burst out again, "It is my new haircut, I can't help how good I look." Samuel smiled and cleared his throat again. He continued, "On behalf of the town council can we accept this term?" Samuel turned and faced everyone, and they all nodded 'yes'. "Ok, on behalf of the town council we accept this term. Now, what is your second term, sir?" Samuel asked trying to hold an air of official decorum. Jova asked, "My last condition is the most important one." In a serious tone he added, "Who decides the level of acting like an ass before I can write a ticket?" The room burst into laughter. All said they would be the judge of assness.

CHAPTER 13

THE KNOT

Several months later, the church was full. Everyone in town was there. As the wedded couple pulled back from a long kiss, they turned and faced the crowd. The pastor spoke with great pride, "Ladies and Gentlemen, I present to you Jova and Sally Zarn." Sally had a big smile and happiness poured from her. Jova's solemn small grin began to grow and grow into uncontrolled laughing. He looked into the audience and the faces came into focus. Each face was different, but there was something in common they all shared. All the smiling men had the same exact big boy haircut as Jova had. From that vantage point, Jova was the only one who noticed. He turned and pulled Sally to him and kissed her again and as he hugged her close, he whispered in her ear, "I love you and thank you for helping a broken man." Tears fell from her eyes as she hugged him back.

The audience erupted in cheers and applause. As the bride and groom breached the grand doors of the church, a group of bystanders threw birdseed on to them and congratulated them. They stopped at the bottom of the steps. A lovely little girl caught Sally's eye. She wore a beautiful little white dress with white stockings and shiny little shoes. The little girl skipped down the sidewalk beside the church. Jova caught on to what Sally saw and instead of getting into the limo, Jova led Sally by the hand and they followed the little girl. The little girl went from a skip to a run straight to the playground. Up to the sliding board, she went, and down she came, with the biggest smile anyone has ever had.

Jova's hand softly caressed Sally's stomach as Sally's face radiated with happiness. Jova led Sally to the swings and placed her on one of them and began to push her back and forth. Her legs went straight, and her head looked back to him. Kids screaming and giggling began to surround them. More kids flooded into the playground area. Parents and guests surrounded the playground as all watched with glee at the children playing. Some parents had that worried look that their kid would get dirty. Some pointed and laughed telling others about their kid playing. A father, proudly rubbing his wife's shoulder, reassured her, "It's ok, let them get dirty, they are fine, they are happy, and they are safe. What more is there?" The wife caressed his hand and leaned her cheek on it.

In the crowd, men's voices began to come clear "That's a good haircut." "I was going to say the same about yours." The conversations on that same topic were peppered throughout the crowd. Peck asked his mother, "I thought they were supposed to go to a reception and then a special place for their honeymoon?" His mom grasped his hand in hers, and her husbands too. "They are in a special place right now, believe me." Peck looked puzzled and asked her, "I thought special places were like Hawaii, Paris, or Rome?" The mother smiled and glanced at her husband and then turned to Peck, "Sweetie, it is not where you go that makes a place special, it's the people you're with that make it special." She gave Peck a kiss on his cheek. She smiled and looked on at Jova smiling, as he pushed Sally with her feet up and leaning back with a big grin on her face.

William was under a pile of kids trying to hold him down. He was yelling, "You got me, you got me!" Janie was standing nearby, directing the kids "Get him and hold him down, officers! He has been naughty, and you need to hold him until he promises to buy everyone ice cream!" William let out a loud playful "NOOOOOOOO-OOO!!!!" All the kids said, "YESSSSSSSSS!!!"and back and forth they yelled, "NOOOOOO!!", "YESSSSSSS!!!" until William finally gave in. "Ok, ok I give up you guys win " "YAAAAAYYYYY" the kids Yelled as they all pushed and pulled William to his feet.

Just then the ice cream truck pulled up in the church parking lot. All the kids surrounded the truck window. "ICE CREAM, ICE CREAM" they yelled. The screams fell silent once all the kids had ice cream. All the parents had ice cream too. William waved Peck over and handed him two ice creams "Please run these over to the bride and groom who are still swinging. Peck replied "Yes Sir"

William rubbed Janie's shoulder and said, "I expect big things from a fine young man like that." Janie nuzzled into his side and said, "I bet", and she kissed his cheek and said, "I am glad you didn't have a problem with the ice cream thing." He kissed her back and said, "Why would I have a problem with kids eating ice cream?" As everyone fell back, the other side of the ice cream truck came in to view with a sign that said, 'JANIE'S VEGAN ICE CREAM MMMMMMMMMM GOOD LIKE SUGAR KISSES'

William laughed out loud, "Yep, I think Peck has a sweet future in front of him." Janie smiled and asked, "Why is that?" William replied, "I heard he just won a college scholarship from a new emerging company."

Jova and Sally sat side by side on the swings eating their ice cream. One hand holding ice cream the other holding each other's hand, gently swinging back and forth.

THE END